As long
As
I love You…

I will let you hurt me

As long As I love You...

I will let you hurt me

Nikhil Mahajan

Srishti
PUBLISHERS & DISTRIBUTORS

SRISHTI PUBLISHERS & DISTRIBUTORS
N-16, C. R. Park
New Delhi 110 019
srishtipublishers@gmail.com

First published by Srishti Publishers & Distributors in 2011

All characters in this book are fictitious, and any resemblance to real persons, living or dead, is coincidental.

Typeset in AGaramond 12pt. by Suresh Kumar Sharma at Srishti

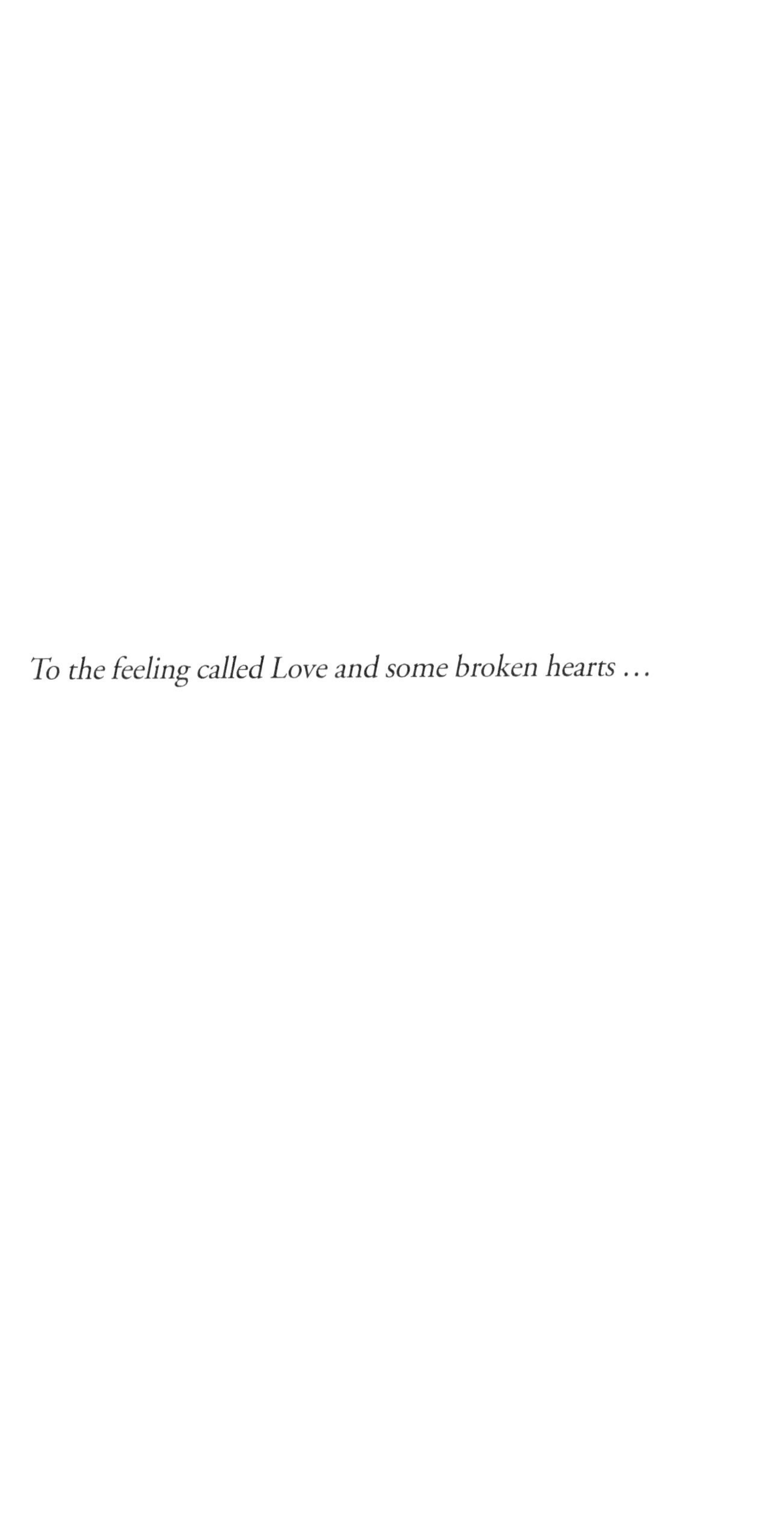

To the feeling called Love and some broken hearts . . .

Acknowledgements

I would like to thank my "Bade Papa" and the other two pillars of my family, "Daddy Papa" and "Nikke papa"; who have always supported me, who have always believed in my dreams and my thoughts. I may not be a perfect child but I try to follow the vision they have of my future and I will always respect it, whatever I do.

I would like to acknowledge my readers for motivating me to write another love story and showering me with their love and support.

A special thanks to my bro, sis and all members of Mahajan family for supporting this effort and working with me on this platform which has always been a dream of mine.

Well! I would like to thank my lil' sweet gf who taught me the meaning of both , the great feeling of love and the tremendous experience of breaking up with someone , which made me stronger and changed a hell a lot of me. I would like to apologize to her as I could not make it up to her, but the promises I had made will never be broken up and I will keep them like a true gentle man.

Her last words to me were –"Don't hope". My answer to that will always remain the same – "Why I should not hope when I believe in myself and I trust in Him : GOD"

Thanks to all the ladies who helped me all along the way with the sweet memories and a specially thanks to that lady who introduced me to my true love knowing that if I get what I desire I'll leave her. I am still buried under the pile of her sacrifices…

Would also like to talk about my mates "Vickey", "Varun", "Amit", "Sunil", "Aman" and "Jai" who have journeyed with me all the way from my breakup, rejections etc to accepting me as I am…

Hat's off to Candy for reviewing the book and giving their useful suggestions, eliminating the mistakes and flaws and making my work more interesting.

I would like to thank my editor and "Srishti Publications" for giving me a chance to introduce myself to this world of words and "Jayanda" ... thank you, for teaching me how to live in this self centered world...

Again a hearty thanks to all who discouraged me to write this book, as they thought such a manuscript might strain a lot of my relations, but one cannot hope for a bright future unless it is based on the foundation of truth.

"To God, for always being there and blessing me with a roof under stormy skies."

Life is not what we always want or predict it to be. After being unnoticed for my work, it was hard for me to swallow that the story was actually stolen by my friend and who did not even acknowledge me.

In the hotel's washroom

Looking into the mirror I could see a d**k head looking straight into my eyes with a piss-off manner saying "Yes! You have ruined it."

For the past some time, I was writing something for Priya, my gf; since our relationship was unstable and things we're not going very well between us. It was my last attempt to show her how I felt. My feelings, put down in ink, took the form of a novel. And on my last meeting with Priya, a thought clicked in my mind. I went to my friend's place and told him my idea of publishing my love life. But my luck had something else in store for me. I showed that manuscript to my friend for proof reading, who got it published under his name and is thus making money off my idea. I could not do anything other than convincing myself that life fucks you up in unexpected ways.

As the saying goes-"you can change anything in this world, but not your bad luck".

Prologue

I called him a million times and finally he decided to meet me once to discuss this issue. This was a bad phase of my life and I had to keep battling things that went wrong.

Lounge Bar, 47 Park Avenue Hotel, Delhi. It was all dark and I could just see a red light seeping through the little space between the edges of the doors. I entered inside and went into the bar. It was all dark and damp. There was a soft song playing in God knows what language. Everyone seemed to be busy with their drinks. The atmosphere in the place was unusually morbid. It seemed like all the DevDs across the country had gathered at the same place for a reunion and I was now a part of it. I took a corner table and within no time I ordered 2 shots of something they called as a death drink. The order took 2 minutes to reach the table, I gulped it downed and it seared my throat as it went down. It worked instantaneously and breathing became heavier and my vision blurred. I decided to go to the washroom.

@ the bar's washroom

Splashing water on my face, I looked at myself in the mirror and expected something better this time. I kept thinking about what I would say to my friend. He knew that it was something very close to my heart; still he did not hesitate in breaching my trust and doing something so despicable.

I looked at my watch; it was time for me to go outside and face everything. The thought of facing him, knowing how much I hated him, was repulsive to me.

Beep

{The phone rings}

The sound of the call diverted my mind, I took out my mobile and looked at its screen; it was his message saying he was waiting outside for me. I didn't want to talk to anyone at that moment except him. It was something that I had to do. I had to tell him how wrong he was.

After I broke up with Priya, this book was the only reminder I had of our love and I could not let anybody take it away from me.

I was screwed but not fucked...

I came out and took the same corner table .My eyes kept looking at the door waiting for him to enter. The door opened and there he was:

Ah! My best friend...

CHAPTER 0
FROM NO WHERE

Well Zero was invented by an Indian and is a number of great significance. I too share a great relation with zero in my life; my mark sheets always had a lot of zeros in them and now as you can notice the Chapter Zero has been introduced in this book.

++ Some wise words: Zero when put in before a number means nothing but if you put this zero at the end of that very number it increases its value. I was the Zero put before a number and so, was of no use++

Playing pranks with everyone, unintentionally hurting everyone, I never noticed when things took a bad turn.

@Hostel no. 5

"Open the door bloody bastard I will kill you"; Kartika cried out in anger.

"***Sale!*** Will break it and will break you too"; he continues and bangs the door with his fist and with his foot hitting hard on the door to break it.

Even though the doors were not very strong, this particular door was doing a pretty good job of keeping me safe.

"***Abbe Ja***"; I replied back rudely from inside, knowing I was safe behind the door.

"Krishna why don't you talk to this bastard about what he did to me; after all you are a friend, his favorite senior" said Kartika to Krishna.

"Whatever it is, it is your problem man. And what has actually happened"? asked Krishna.

"He is a bastard"; said Kartika aloud so that I too could hear him.

I put on a song at the loudest possible volume, to irritate him.

Song played: "I am too sexy for my shirt too sexy by: Right said Fred"

I too sang along with the song to irritate Kartika standing outside.

"You will come to know when you will fall in love Manav"; replied Kartika.

"You know you are a dog"; he continued.

"WOOH WOOH"; I barked from inside to irritate him more.

"Do you think I will ever"; I replied back and you know why "Coz I am too sexy for your GF to be sexy for your Ex too sexy and

I am gonna leave all…" I just sang along with song.

I kept singing and Kartik kept beating the door from outside in anger. I knew if by chance the door broke Kartika would kill me.

I lay on the bed smiling; the drama was ended when Krishna took Kartika out for a fag so that he could calm down and so my skin was saved.

Krishna had always been a rescuer for me because I kept making ***Bakra*** out of people and they kept threatening to break my bones.

Rings

"Hey dude Binnie here, Mani it was awesome; ***sale!*** How do you think of this witty stuff? "; said Binnie, another defaulter and my partner in this prank, calling me up to congratulate me on what I did in the college that morning.

"Yeah I know I know" I replied back in confidence, patting my own back.

"I bow to you man, we all bow to you; ***tu kameena hai"***; Binnie said, giving me a compliment.

"Yeah dude I have to be out of Kartika's sight for few days, he's so angry. He said he was truly in love with this gal with whom we just played the prank"; I replied back, giving a warning to Binnie so that he could also be safe.

"Take a chill-pill" replied Binnie, ensuring me of his safety.

—@—

Few hours earlier: In the morning

We were in Miss. Sehgal's class. Everyone was fond of this class. Suddenly…

"I need a favor"; said Kartika to me while I was busy in the class.

I was just looking at Miss. Sehgal's beauty and was drawing her curves in my note book with my pencil. She was awesome as ever. I had a crush on her. With every movement she made, she looked prettier than ever.

"What man"; I replied back as Kartika distracted me from my fantasy.

"I have a crush on a girl from my dance class and I want you to call her up as me and convince her to meet me somewhere. You know I am no good at talking to girls", he explained.

"I am not the right person to help you out. You have knocked on the wrong door, dear" I replied back as I was also in the same condition. I felt very shy in front of gals. LOL.

"Otherwise I would had proposed Gauri"; said I to Kartika.

"You mean our senior Gauri?" replied Kartika, his mouth hanging open in surprise.

"What?" said I.

"Gauri???" Kartika replied back.

"Nah"; I tried to act as if the name suddenly came out of my mouth and now I was hiding it.

"Leave it, I'll talk to Binnie to help you out"; I tried flipping the topic.

Bell rang and the lecture got over. I move out and Kartika followed me all the way.

"Binnie"; I called Binnie from the crowd.

"Yeah dude" replied back Binnie raising his hand up like a dude.

"I need a favor, I mean Kartika needs it. Talk to this gal on the phone and call her somewhere." I looked at Kartika to tell me the spot.

"Well canteen"; Kartika said.

"Kartika is in love"; I stared into Binnie's eyes and he knew I was up to something.

"Ok man, what the big deal. You came at the right place"; said Binnie to Kartika, putting his hand on his shoulder and taking him away from me to the porch.

"Who is this girl?" enquired Binnie while taking him out to the balcony this time and showing his interest in the matter.

"My crush. Here in this college but in some other stream. I saw her in Dance Classes"; Kartika uttered like a baby crying out for a toy in a store, excitedly.

"Call her up and stop enquiring man"; I ordered Binnie while handing him my mobile.

Kartika gave the number to Binnie and…

Rings

"Hi this is Kartika here and I hope you don't have any lecture right now and I am not disturbing you, calling you at this hour"; said Binnie confidently.

"Yeah may I know who this is at the other side? I don't talk to strangers"; enquired the girl.

"C'mon I am Kartika from you Dance Classes and I was thinking…" replied Binnie.

"Who??" asked the girl, confused.

"We should meet somewhere. You know I am a huge fan of your dancing and my dad is working with some of the good Dance shows in the entertainment industry and he can help you out if you are really interested in making your dancing career"; said Binnie, all in one breath so that it made an impact on the girl and I knew he was a lying, man he was uttering anything which came into his mind like a script.

"Awesome"; came from my mouth.

The idea of recommendation gave Kartika a chance to make out with the girl and a cup of coffee.

"Whenever you are free I am ready to meet you"; said girl.

"So meet me in an hour in the canteen"; said Binnie being Kartika.

Kartika was awed at how easily Binnie convinced the girl.

"Look it's done. Now go meet your girl"; said Binnie to Kartika.

I opened Facebook on my mobile and started searching for the girl.

"What should I do now"; said Kartika to me asking for further assistance.

"How can I tell you? I don't know anything, I never had a girl friend"; I reply back to Kartika.

"Be ready to meet your dream girl. Do nothing, you just tuck in your shirt man, at least show some respect to the first meeting"; said Binnie while we started moving towards the canteen.

"We will sit on the next table. Just relax and don't look at us"; said Binnie.

"I am not going"; I said, being a little scared.

"Go to the washroom and make yourself presentable"; I said to Kartika pointing towards the washroom.

"Okie you wait here"; said Kartika heading towards the washroom.

As soon as Kartika entered the loo I latched it from outside.

"What are doing man?" said Binnie looking at me.

"Man just look at this girl. She is awesome and you want this bloody Kartika to be with her who doesn't even know how to talk to girls and is asking us for help. Man, she needs you... she needs you..."; said I to Binnie with a cunning smile on my face and he knew I had planned something mischievous in my mind which needs execution as soon as it gets Binnie's approval.

"So"; asked Binnie unaware of my intentions and plan.

"Just call the girl again, ask her out but tell her this time that the plan has changed. Call her to meet you at the Nescafe outside the campus"; I suggest Binnie handing him my mobile for the call and putting our plan into action.

After a few rings the girl picked up.

"Hello, Ya this is Kartika here. I have some urgent work so can we meet now? I mean if it is okay with you"; said Binnie to the girl as soon as she picked up the call.

"Yeah! Hmm.... Lemme see whether I have a class, gimme 2 min I will call you"; replied the girl and disconnected.

We knew ***vo thoda bhav kha rahi thi*** but still.

Reply came as a SMS after some time: "Ya sure"

We headed towards the Nescafe leaving Kartika there latched in the washroom.

"Run"; said I to Binnie and in a minute we reached the place. The girl was already there waiting for us.

"Who is gonna be Kartika now?" said Binnie.

"Of course you, man I am not a Stud man! My status about girls is same as Kartika. So it makes no difference"; said I, permitting Binnie to make a move.

Reaching near girl we made an entry from behind.

"Hi" said Binnie to the girl, waving his hand.

"Hello" respond the girl with a smile and both shook hands.

"Hey this is my friend Manav" pointing towards me and introducing me.

I raised my hand, like taking an oath. "Hi" with a smile.

And the two started talking about dance and I kept an eye on the road for Kartika.

An hour passed and I was getting bored with the two love birds totally ignoring me. Aw... Binnie was too good at ***pataoing*** girls and I was just a newbie in this business. Suddenly I saw Kartika screaming aloud and heading towards us.

"Run Binnie Run"; said I to Binnie as I prepared myself to run.

Before I could utter anything more; Binnie without replying started running towards the other side of the road. I ran as fast as I could to save myself and I headed towards the hostel whereas Binnie ran towards his PG.

As I looked back while running, I saw Kartika going back to the girl who was watching everything confused.

"I am Kartik"; said Kartika to the silly girl introducing himself. He was huffing and puffing like a steam engine.

"Who were they?" asked the girl confused.

"My friends, oh I mean I don't know them, just bastards…fooling around"; said Kartika to the girl

"I don't know what kinda prank is this but it is making me really angry. Better get out of my sight who so ever you are"; said girl angrily.

Kartika tried hard to convince the girl that he was not at fault, but in vain.

I safely reached my hostel and bolted the door.

CHAPTER 1
INTRO

The hostel was a place of distractions, and never a place to study. Me and Rohit, we had an ***adda*** for studying, yet I was not so good at it but for the sake of our parents we used to study on Rohit's terrace. It was chosen because from there we could have good view of all the girls in the neighborhood. Girls- a life line to all the boys. I and Rohit had our territories demarcated. I had one end of the neighbor and I had rights over the girls on that side where as Rohit held the other side.

It was followed by me and Rohit. Until Meha came...

Well, I am Manav, 19 years old physiotherapy, 1st year student, jolly by nature and ready to do mischief.

For me life was like an ice-cream, you have to eat it before it melts. I never knew something like love can ever happen to me. Until, I saw Meha, I saw this girl for the first time, I don't remember much but she had waist length hair. She was like a blossoming Lilly flower, just so fresh and pretty. She was as perfect as could imagine.

One cannot stop himself from loving her. She was the one I had always dreamt about.

@

——First sight——

Who says there is no love at first sight? Yes it was love at the first sight.

It is true; I fell in love with this girl at the first glance. Her innocence just struck me like lightening. She was the first love of my life. As I saw this girl from the balcony with her wet hair I was struck with cupid's arrow. Eventually I became addicted with watching her.

Watching her at all times became my life's motive. I started visiting Rohit's terrace everyday so that I could get a good look at her and admire her beauty. I would follow her to the market, would run into her intentionally by mistake. I did everything to make her notice me but there was no response.

It was now a one sided love. I tried my best. I tried talking to her younger brother; tried to make him my friend; that was all I kept doing for some months. I gave her brother any number of bribes but nothing worked. Her mom was known to me but she had no idea of my intentions for her daughter. So going directly to her was a tough job here.

——The start——

Days passed with no satisfactory result but still the spark of creating a rapport with her kept burning. I had given up my earlier ways of making fun of everybody and being insensitive.

I never knew this could happen to guy like me. But then, love does come uninvited. Does it not?

I would park my scooter in front of her house, trying to get a glimpse of her. I would smile at her anytime I saw her. But she never responded.

And then one day I got lucky. She made a move.

One day I parked my scooter in front of her house and walked to Rohit's place. I saw her and smiled at her. But again she was expressionless like a stone. I was a little hurt like always. I was trying so hard and she did not give a damn. Also I could not be too blatant as our parents knew each other and she could simply call my dad and tell him what I was doing, if she so pleased.

That day when I came back to my scooter I saw some little stickers glued to my scooter's seat. They were a boy and a girl sticker. They were the silliest thing one could have done in love. When I pulled them off there was a phone number underneath, with time, when to call. I could have died of happiness then and there.

Rings

With a single ring, Meha picked up the call from the other end.

"Hello"; muttered the girl from the other side with a sweet soft voice. Her mother or sister was there at the same room or may be close to her.

"Hi"; I said being a little formal.

"Who is this?" I enquire.

"Meha"; she said.

"Ok me Manav here at other end."

"I know I gave you my number and the time"; said the girl a lil louder, to be audible enough.

"Ya"; I was little confused and scared thinking maybe I was being tricked.

As I was new to this, I had no idea what to say.

The silence remained constant for about a minute, as we both had nothing to speak.

"Ok now I have to put down the line Manav"; said Meha.

Still with so much from her side I could not say anything to her.

"Well would you meet me outside tomorrow?" I suddenly asked.

"I will think over it and then I will give you time when to call me again. Then I will tell you." said Meha while putting down the line.

The conversation ended. And our affair d'amour began.

In a day or two I got the chance to meet the girl.

@

——Call——

Love was a new thing in the life to think over and Meha was fully contributing to it. The relation was founded, only some good times were needed to be shared and Meha was ready for it. But I suffered from constant nausea simply because of fear.

Rings

"Hello" said the familiar voice.

"Hello" said I.

"It's me Meha"; said the girl.

"Oh hi Meha how come you called me up"; I questioned.

"You know what my friend just went for a date with her boy friend"; the girl uttered everything as if she was very excited about it.

"Then what"; replied I, in a casual way but my heart was pounding and I was crossing my fingers thinking that she might also ask me to take her out; as I knew nothing what to do on a date and I didn't want my first date to be failure.

Moreover I had already heard from my friends that girls and boys do kiss each other, hold hands.

This was something I could not do in the public as I was shy kind of guy.

"Manav c'mon be a sport, *yaar*, I am telling you all this so that we can also meet." girl said in a very loveable way that I could not bring myself to say no to her words.

"May be sometime, wait for the right time"; said I being a stud like I am not like those guys who are charged up to meet their girl, being cheesy with them and date them for thing called SEX.

Yes sex was something missing from my life and was something I was unaware of and it seems to be mandatory if you are in love with someone.

"May be at the end of the month or the first week of the next month"; I replied convincing the girl while looking at my pocket.

My pockets were empty and were not up to the mark for facing the expenditure and it was needed that we have to wait for the whole month so that I can get my pocket money.

CHAPTER 2

MY FIRST DATE

Finally the day of my first date ever came. I had gained enough courage and enough knowledge about the concept of a perfect date.

To perform well onsite, I took a 3-day crash course from my playboy friend, Karan. He, of course, wanted reimbursement in the form of beer.

So we decided to meet at a restaurant close to her home. I followed some basics of the crash course. Politeness was the key major and the gift was the key minor.

And I brought a gift with me which Karan helped me in choosing. I entered the restaurant where my girl was waiting for me. She was wearing a pink top and blue jeans which fit her perfectly and she was looking beautiful as ever. Lights were dim. An instrumental song was playing and the atmosphere was so ambient that even a person who was not in love can enjoy the moment. We took our seat but I was rather shy because of my inexperience.

Everything was going well. I made my decided move.

To start the conversation I said, "So what would you like to have?"

To my question, Meha just nodded her head as if she also felt shy and we both could not make eye contact with each other.

But it was necessary for the flow so I in a casual way, hiding my nervousness, asked Meha again.

"Should I order something for you myself?" I stood up without looking at Meha, went to the counter to place an order and hide my nervousness.

"Cold drinks and burger for two"; said I to the cashier.

Paying the amount and taking the slip for my drink I came back to the table.

To make the meeting more purposeful I started the conversation again, "So, are you feeling shy?"

"Ya" said Meha.

"Me too", said I.

"You are also a first timer"; said Meha to my words.

"No" said I to save my skin and to be a dude in front of her.

Ring

I took the call; it was my brother who was calling me.

"Hey Manav where are you?" asks my elder brother as I picked up the call.

"Where is my car?" he continued.

"I have an urgent piece of work at college so I took your car, so why don't you take my bike, keys are there on the table"; I replied to him and convinced him that I need the car and he should go out on my bike.

"Ok" said bro "But you try to make it fast to home and don't roam here and there."

"Sure"; reply I, dropping down the line.

To start the conversation again, I gave a start.

"Meha" I called her name to get her attention.

"So what was your score in your 10th standard"; I asked Meha.

And this was the most idiotic question one could ask on their first date. Due to nervousness my IQ level was dropping.

"What"; said Meha, giving an appropriate reaction to my question.

"I mean division"; I asked again while changing the question a bit.

"I mean I am asking you coz I just want to know why you chose non-medical"; this time I made a self answer to my question to cover the embarrassment.

"I like numbers"; said Meha to justify herself here.

I tried diverting this conversation here as it showed my interest in studies, which I hate most. To show her myself uninterested further I started sipping my drink which was just placed on the table. As I took a sip, I heard a familiar voice outside. I could feel something bad was going to happen. My eyes kept noticing the door of the restaurant and Meha kept noticing me.

"What happened, you called someone?" said Meha.

"No"; I replied while continuously looking at the door.

"Then why you are staring at the door and not concentrating on the food"; said Meha to get my attention.

Suddenly the door opened; as I knew something bad was going to happen and to my surprise in came my brother with someone. Looking at my brother scared the hell out of me. I was stunned. A gush of blood ran to my head and I stood up, shot towards the kitchen of the restaurant to save my butt. But I could not find a way out. The situation was helpless.

To make a quick escape and in confusion I ran towards the curtain and hid myself. Meha kept watching the whole drama, with her utter surprise visible on her face. But she could easily make out that something was wrong. She came near the curtains where I was hiding myself and sat on the table next to it.

"Mani can you tell me why you are hiding yourself here in such a silly way"; said Meha in a rather funny manner.

"Hey don't talk so loud"; reply I.

"So can you now tell me what's there on your mind"; whispered Meha with a smile on her face.

"The guy who just entered"; said I.

"Yup the one in a white shirt"; reply Meha.

"Ya that one"; said I.

"Then what"; Meha asked me forcefully so get a clear picture.

"He's my elder brother"; said I.

"So what!" said Meha again?

"If he finds me here with you then he will definitely tell mom and dad and I had just lied to him that I am busy with some urgent work at college"; said I, all in a single breath.

"Then what if he will tell about our date, why don't you tell mom and dad about this before they find it from your brother"; said Meha.

"What do you mean"; I tried to look for my brother this time from inside the curtains.

"The one, with whom he's sitting "; said Meha.

"Isn't he's with a girl" said Meha again.

"And he's with his GF I bet"

"How do you know she's his GF?" I questions Meha.

"Well no one holds hand such a way and look in each other's eye in such a pretty manner and it's so romantic and this could not be the first time like us"; answer Meha.

"You just come out of the curtains, hold my hand and look in to my eyes"; said Meha in a romantic way.

Something just enlightened Meha while looking at my brother and their sweet relationship. This was the key stone to her and to make her understand what is to be done on a date. She also wanted the same. She also wanted me to hold her and look into her eye and say her three pious love words and praise her to as the most beautiful girl in the world.

Her bold words were enough to make me courageous enough to come out of these curtains and in no time before I could change my mind I came out. I hold my girl's hand while looking into her eyes and taking a place just next to her.

But I could hardly look at my brother's side and then after some time I found my brother was gone from the restaurant while I was busy talking with my girl.

May be he felt bad, shy or maybe he was disturbed due to our presence; so he went out.

This thing never came out and neither of us talks about it ever. The thing remains buried into each other's heart. Thus a first date, a first impression of love was made into my life.

Love was in the clouds and rainbows everywhere, we were talking on phone each and every day without thinking that we will get caught on the very day of billing. Who cares at that moment so do I?

Finally her mother got to know about our little cute love story and I came to know that her sister was my classmate and due to this my relation got disturbed.

CHAPTER 3

THE SECOND START

Things were going great with Meha. Life was fine but still something was missing out of it. My heart...

Few years back, I had an Angel in my life- her name was Diva. I always had an avid for her. I knew nothing about her much, just a regular update from my friends that she's going out with someone; guy was a stud - Kabir.

I left the thought about her and continue to glare her whenever I get a chance to, but Meha's presence keep Diva out of my mind. Her company was enjoyable but yet not satisfactory. In my hearts heart a pain for being with Diva was still scratching my wounds. Her house was on the way back to my hostel from Rohit's house.

Still whenever I get time to have a glance of her I could arrange an eye tonic for myself standing in front of her house waiting for this girl to come out at balcony or see her while she goes out or enters her house.

What went wrong with me and Meha was the fact that she wanted romance and I was slowly losing interest. I was slowly realizing that it was mere infatuation and not loves. In the meanwhile, I was falling for a girl called Diva.

Meha kept pressing me to tell her I loved her. I did not want to lie to her and I finally told her that I did not love her and I loved a girl called Diva. Surprisingly, Meha knew Diva and was ready to help me.

+++Some wise words: Whatever a guy thinks about his friend circle; almost every girl knows every other girl and they have a bigger circle than guys++

Phone rings

"Hello"; a girly voice came from other side and was hardly recognizable.

"Hello." I said.

"May I know who is calling"; I continues.

"Ya, this is Diva"; said the girl.

This name shook me up and I got goose bumps with the name. Several thoughts came into my mind. Should I say anything or should I ask her maybe she had dialed a wrong number.

My mind kept on moving from one thought to another but

nothing seemed to make sense.

"Hey you there"; said Diva as I was lost in my thoughts.

"Ya I am here"; I replied back, confused.

"So you like me"; said Diva in a monotonous way, the tone was pinching me and I could hardly see a light of the friendship in that case.

I knew I was screwed up here, but still wanted to make matters clear.

"Ya, I do but how did you come to know about it?" I asked.

"Well I've been told by Meha", here I recognized the voice.

I just came to know I was being tricked by some bitchy girls and my current girlfriend. The girls were laughing in the background and I was just holding my mobile in my hand. And suddenly the thought of Meha caught hold of me. The idiot girl was preparing me more and more with her pranks to overcome the fear of rejection. The prank was nothing more than motivation.

"Why don't you say LOVE YOU to me"; cried Meha.

"Because I like you and at the same time I think I am not really in love with you"; I answered her usual question.

"Are we gonna live like this forever?" said Meha with pain.

"Am I so bad that you can't love me" she continued and her voice had become numb by the time.

"No baby this is just a bad time, you just be with me and we will overcome it together" said I, surrendering myself to her tears.

Such conversations always ended with no results and were now casual between us. With just a long pause and silly silence, I drop the line. Diva was now echoing in my mind, soul, heart and my relation. And this was something which was happening with us every day. She always forced me to say the golden words but every time she argued with me, she just reminded me of Diva and love for her.

Finally Meha made up her mind to make a deal with me.

Late at night the phone rang again.

"Hello"; said a sad voice. May be someone was crying at other end.

"Hello"; replied I.

"I know you don't love me but can I ask you till when it will continue or I should stop expecting"; the voice came from the other end was low as if someone had cried for long and it was Meha who was calling me.

"It's not like that Meha, but why don't you understand that I am not in love"; replied I, defending myself from her allegations.

"No Mani you don't understand" and the words fade away with sobs coming from the other end.

"Will let Diva know about your feelings if you are so desperate for her. At least I can do this for you in love"; and the line was drop down.

I could not sleep the whole night thinking, what Meha is going through when I say I don't love her and what I would have felt if I would have been in her place.

Days passed like this till one day when I got this call in the noon.

Phone rings

It was some unknown number flashing on the mobile. Unaware and unprepared I took the call.

"Hello"; I said in an enquiring manner.

"This is Diva here"; clearing herself at other end the tone was bit angry.

"Ya I know this is a new prank and I don't care about whatever you are thinking I would like to admit; I love you, Yes I do and does this mean anything to you DIVA"; I too sharing the prank my own way.

"What nonsense! It was your girlfriend who forced me to call you and I thoroughly regret it now!"

I could hear a harsh tone and it was confusing because the prank never ended in such way.

I called back at the same number but it turned out to be busy every time. Now I was sure that there was something fishy going on. So I decided to call Meha up.

I dialed Meha's number.

Rings

"Ya Mani"; said Meha from other side.

"Did you call me?" I asked.

"No I didn't." replied Meha innocently.

"Then who called me up with Diva's name"; I said angrily so that if she was still in a mood for cracking some poor joke, she might confess it before the thing get onto my nerves.

"So finally she called you and I hope you convinced her how much you love her"; said Meha, her voice was like she was doing all this for me because she loves me.

"May be"; I put down the line showing her my anger. I knew she'll cry after this act but I could not care less about it.

I called my friend up to check the number so that I can look into the matter; who dared to play such a prank on me. I was still sure that it was someone's mischief. I was used to such prank calls from the past few times so it was hard for me to accept that Diva really called me up.

It was a poor experience that many a times such calls came up from Meha's side and ended very indecently. I was used to all this but what happened that day intrigued me.

Whenever I ask: Who is there at the other end?

The person starts making fun of me. A thought still bothered my mind- Meha could call pretending to be Diva, so believing Meha was also difficult. It was on the regular basis that Meha was now calling me anytime in the day saying this is Diva on the other side.

I called Karan, the rescuer, to help me out. I handed over the number to my spy friend to enquire about the caller and report back to me. It was confirmed that it was Diva who called me. But this time after the real Diva's call, now the missing link between Diva and me was coming into picture. Now all I had to do was impress her.

To do this I had to call her again for a better start but I need some time for it. I waited for the right time, it took few days to prepare so that the bad image could be forgotten and I could concentrate on her. These days were enough for me to get a new start and polish myself to win her heart.

I made statements, I wrote some punch lines and key words on the piece of paper so that I should be well prepared for this girl.

Finally the day came when I decided to call her up.

Rings

"Hello"; said Diva.

"Hello" I replied.

The fear of losing her was there in my heart but still I had to make a move, regaining some courage I started the conversation from my side.

"This is Mani here"; I said.

"I don't remember any…" said diva giving me a cold shoulder and it was true from her part because the incident was now an old story where I was a loser as I could not say anything in my defense.

"Ya I know because I could hardly say anything to you as you called me mad"; I said again thinking may be this time I can make a start.

"Oh am sorry if I had said so but really I don't use such words for strangers"; said the girl in a very fancy way.

"There might be some reason of saying it..." continue her.

"Ya because you got some news about my feelings from someone else and I could hardly defend myself that time as my parents were with me"; I said something I even don't know, unprepared.

"Parent's" I talk to myself... for... I was confused and that was the only thing I could remember that time.

"Oh! Then I am really sorry to create trouble for you"; said Diva in an apologizing way.

"Hey no, it's not like that, I have just recently been through a breakup with my girlfriend and as she asks me whom I love in real I said your name, Diva. I took you name..."; I said all without thinking about the consequences if Meha will ever know.

I was waiting for the line to be disconnected.

Nothing happened...

"What kind of joke is this, are you nuts, I still don't know you"; said the girl, this time she seemed to be a little pissed.

"Look this might be annoying for you but I love you, ever since I saw you", I continued.

"This is something I've been doing for a long time now"

"And yes it is true I used to see you, from school to tuitions, I was all there. I was out of your sight, but no one can question my existence in your life. I was searching for information about you from my friends"; I said it all as it was now last chance for me.

"So you are saying just because you were stalking me, I am now obligated to love you"; said Diva angrily.

"Look I would not like to disturb you Diva and I should have not told you all this in this life time but since you might have heard from someone else, so I decided to call you up and tell you my feelings in my own way"; I said.

"I would have confessed it earlier in front of you but I didn't want to disturb you as you were busy with your boyfriend and your love life"; I said all together, like a speech to impress her.

"Don't talk about him"; said Diva.

There was something… fishy… I guess… and I could sniff some kind of behavioral charge when I talked about her boyfriend.

"What happened, why you sound so upset?" I said.

"Look I don't have to talk to you much now, so be kind to me and if you really love me I would rather suggest you please don't call me again, I will be highly obliged"; said the girl while putting down the line.

I was all drowned in my own world. I kept recalling the things we had said in our lil' chit-chat on the phone and trying to figure out what I had probably said that made her put down the line.

Everything was on track. This method had passed the test of time and had never failed before. I called Karan my spy friend to rescue me again.

Rings

"Hey Karan I need some more info about the girl"; I said while Karan listened to me quietly.

"About her routine work and her boy friend, as soon as possible man"; I said.

"Ok man chill out! What conversation did you people have?" Karan asks me.

"Nothing just she did not stay on the line longer and didn't give me a chance to say anything"; I reply in pain.

"Ok I am keeping your issue high on my priority list"; Karan said proudly as if he was the only love boy around and banged down the line.

I waited till the evening when Karan messaged me.

I opened my Inbox:

"Bro bad news for you, you called her up at a bad time, she's having a bad time with her boyfriend"

I read the message and found myself fooled again but this time by my destiny. I wondered why everything was going wrong whenever I tried to link up with Diva. I was just breaking up with each catch.

I messaged Karan: "What kinda bad times"

Reply came: "About to break up"

I was bit happy for myself and sad for Diva. There was a mixed confused feeling about the situation. Things seem to be on track for me but what about Diva.

BAD was the word I had in my mind for her.

I repeatedly called Diva but she refused to be my friend either. Time came when I was no longer in contact with Diva and my gf Meha.

It was a hard time for me and my exams were just around the corner.

++ Some wise words: Every successful person has a lady behind him, and its true when you leave the lady behind, you'll definitely get the success++

So I was following these wise words. I was busy with exams while Karan was busy with Diva and Meha and without my knowledge was helping me all the way to go through my love life.

Sometimes it is helpful in getting closer to someone when you make some negative image in others eyes.

Karan, my friend, was secretly cutting my throat. The man was working on Diva so that he could get her and I being unaware to his intentions was ignoring this girl as well as my girl.

Now the time came when my exams got over and it was the party time but my hands were empty, my girl and Diva both were missing from my life.

++ Some wise words by some wise men: Only good and bad is noticeable, rest all goes unrecognized++

I had 39 messages beeping on my mobile and all were unread. I knew some of them were from Meha and surprisingly some were Diva's messages.

I opened the last message to start.

It was Meha's message: "Mani I got caught at home, my father had read all the cards you gave to me and he's angry about it and searching for you. So please stay away from my place".

It was something about which I didn't felt sad while reading the message and rather I was happy that Meha is not going to disturb me for few days. Whereas it gives me enough time to make it up with Diva now.

But where was Diva, she was missing. I searched in my message box so that I could see any message received from her.

I found her message, it was Diva's last message, might be the last for this life as her message made me upset "I came to know about you; if you were so much serious about me... but you are like other guys around"

"Being with someone for some time and now same as ignoring them"

It was disappointing for me.

I knew the girl's messenger ID all I had to do was search her when she was online and had to be with her again.

I called her up but she stopped picking up my calls.

I left a mail to the lady saying sorry and saying that I was bit busy with the examination and that was the reason that I could not call her and ignored her.

No message came from the other side and I still waited for the mail with a hope. I tried her mobile number many a times till I got a message from her side which was rather confusing, talking about my relationship with Meha. Putting some effort to my social calculations, I realized someone had bitched to her about me. I knew Meha would not do such a thing at this moment of time so it must be someone else. I finally came to a conclusion that it must be Karan who had done the back stabbing act.

So I tried to call her up and before calling her I made a decision to message her, to trick her into picking up my call for the last time.

And after the delivery message I called her up.

It was a sad moment and I knew I had lost everything. I had no feelings for Meha but by the time I was messaging Diva I was sure that I really loved her from the core of my heart and I had only one single chance to admit it to her. Things were balanced on the edge word and it could have happened for us or it could have ended, once and for all.

To my surprise before I could call Diva, the call came from the other end itself.

"Hello"; said Diva from other side.

"Ya Diva this is me Mani, dear I know you must be angry with me"; I said.

"I am sorry Mani I misunderstood you and believed Karan's words which confused me"; said Diva and her words were little confusing and I could not understand what had actually happened in my favor.

"What are you talking about"; I made a move.

"I called Meha up and asked about yours and her relation..." Diva said.

My breath got heavy and many thoughts haunted my mind that actually what conversation happened between the two ladies of my life.

"And...?" I could utter this much only

"She said she is just your friend nothing else and I am sorry about messaging you all that, all because of Karan"; said Diva apologetically.

I was a bit surprised at hearing Meha's words.

Might be her dad or may be some other reason; maybe for sake of my happiness she made this sacrifice. But I was happy and that was much more important.

Days passed so easily, I came close to Diva while Meha was struggling with her family to overcome trauma caused by my name, till the day came when I gave a letter to Diva, expressing my emotions for her.

POEM: A new beginning A new Journey

Life is not the way we expect
It has So many twists and turns
One way leading to other with churns
Just like a cold freeze with cold burns

So many pebbles on the road
leading to other as we board
It's no wonder
that some may lose their way
and some just distracts
until they are left behind on the track

But we have not to look back...

Should we cry for the lost
and those who fall behind?
Or this journey keeps on
should we stop and wait?

I choose to walk alone on my path.
When you try to catch up, I was all gone
walking beside me just was a dream

Something like desert you can't win

Love was something

That can't happen here.

I was lost all wear and tear...

So, I begin with
A new beginning. A new journey...

MANAV

CHAPTER 4

LOVE: OH NO! NOT AGAIN

Days passed like that and I could not say anything to Diva. I wanted a start now. One day on the way from college to the home I tracked Diva and messaged her that lets talk somewhere. Finally, I met Gill, my friend, on the way to home. Gill was a University singer and was a guitarist too. Gill was my hope for Diva out here. I managed to get introduced to Gill for the plan execution. I wanted to propose Diva with a song. I arranged everything for the date and the proposal song composed and well tuned. It took a month for me and Gill to prepare our little performance.

@

—Sunday—-

It was Sunday and colleges were closed. In the morning, I called up Diva a lot of times but her number was busy so I called up Gill to cancel the plan till next Sunday.

Love was travelling through my blood and I could not resist myself. Finally after all endless efforts Diva call me up in the noon.

"What's up Mani? I am busy with my assignments"; said Diva.

"I know but I want to meet you"; said I.

"I can't meet you today, I am busy with my assignments and I am going to the cybercafé for checking my emails"; reply Diva.

"Which café ?" I enquire.

"What you want to do Mani? Are you spying on me?"

"I also planned to check my email so it's better, I will also come over there and we can meet too"; I said planning up for a second chance.

"No! You are not coming over there"; said Diva closing the chapter.

"Ok, is that clear"; said Diva while moving out of her house and calling up an auto rickshaw.

"Sector 21"; said Diva to auto rickshaw driver and the call ended.

It was the only sign I needed to reach the place where my angel was going. So without any thought I went out for the sector 21.

On the way I called her again to check that she had not changed the plan.

Rings

"Where are you? Can we meet?" I said.

"I am at the café Mani please stop irritating me like a kid." Diva replies back.

After a half hour drive I finally reached the café where Diva was supposed to be checking her mails.

@

—Cyber café—-

Before I could start with my date we had a fight which was settled down by the café owner.

I told Diva to take a cabin and I paid for two cabins. Diva looked at me and what I was doing.

"We are together here now for which you just had fight and I think we should share a single cabin." said Diva staring me.

I knew the Gill plan was messed up so I had to compromise here with some other thing.

"Well you check your email"; I replied back getting rescued from the sharing and caring thing.

"Ok as you wish "; said Diva disappointed while moving towards her cabin.

I entered the cabin next to her cabin and opened my messenger there and waited till she came online.

I knew if she opens her email, she will definitely log on to messenger too. I waited for 5 minutes till her ID flashed: online on the screen.

"Hi"; I type and press enter.

"Hi"; Diva replies back.

"ASL plz"; I type back, for which Diva too replied in a fashionable way.

And the conversation started and Diva started enjoying this strange game.

"I was gazing at you for the past few years, if you had noticed I was there all the time even though I was missing from your life"; I typed and this time the chat became a lil' serious.

"And I knew when you had a BF and I never tried to interfere in your relationship"; I typed

"Well I had also chatted with you many times with different IDs if you remember"; I typed, all with the screen names using which I used to chat with her.

These things were shocking for the girl and the game was turning serious with each word I typed. These were not only the words; they were the truth I was admitting in front of her. This game was intentionally planned. I knew I could not tell her all this while facing her. So I decided this was the best way I could admit and also see her reaction.

"Hm..." only this message came back from other side.

"And it's been 3 years I've been gazing at you and when you came into my life as a friend. But all is changed now"

"Tell me how is it my fault if I entered your life so late?" I typed all on her ID without looking at the answers.

Nothing came this time. The chat had stopped. I got scared that my ***bindaasgiri*** this time had put me into trouble and also the newly formed friendship.

"You there?" I typed.

Still nothing came from the other side. I tried to peep from my cabin into her cabin to look at her face, whether she is angry or not. I could not see her. She was gone leaving her ID open there on the screen.

"Diva"; I shouted aloud in the café.

"Ya Mani"; said Diva from one side near the printer.

"Sorry I am getting my paper printed lemme finish it then we will chat again"; said Diva looking at me and pointing towards the printed sheets.

I ran towards her cabin and with no time I close our chat window where I was admitting all the silly things.

"What are you doing?" asks Diva entering the cabin.

"Nothing" I reply her back turning back and hiding the computer screen.

My skin was just safe as I just closed the chat window. I smiled from inside for my idiotic act.

"My cabin's computer was slow, so I thought while you are getting your sheets printed I will check messenger here on your computer"; said I covering the whole drama.

"Ok you stay here I will use that node, hardly matters I had checked my email"; said Diva while moving out of cabin.

Suddenly I remember that the chat is still opened there on my computer screen for which I just came to close here in her cabin. I was going to wreck the situation and I had to control it as soon as possible.

"No I will use mine"; said I while I try to push myself in the small cabin and moving out.

"You are acting wired" said Diva, getting a little pissed off with me.

I ran towards my cabin and switched off my node's screen.

"Are you looking at porn or what, why are you sweating so much?" said Diva looking at me in a suspicious way and being very straight.

This was enough for me to create a little mess and to escape from the question answer round.

"Do I look like person who is into these all this stuff"; said I angrily.

"No I was just joking Mani I didn't mean that"; said Diva back.

"Leave it let's go from here. We will not stay here"; I said in a bossy manner and we moved out to have coffee. The coffee shop was near the Café in sector 21 only. Ambience was just perfect and was the decided place by me and Gill for our little performance but plan was just postponed.

@

—Coffee shop—-

"Mocha for two"; said Diva to the waiter while I came from the washroom.

"So you were spying on me?" asks Diva with a smile.

"No I don't do such things" I reply with an eye raised.

"Porn" asked Diva mischievously.

"You didn't even let me enter your cabin"

"Tell me ***na*** Mani what you were doing in my cabin"; Diva started the same conversation again.

"Ah nothing"; said I.

And I went to the counter to see the other labels there. Diva remained seated at her place.

As it was the place for the performance of our little show but I forgot to tell the Café owner that the plan had been cancelled. They decorated the place in the way they were told and the act started unintentionally the way it was planned. Flowers came into the scene as I made my first move and took my seat. I was shocked as it was the first act of the plan. I now could not say no to it so I made a move stood up and kneeling down gave the flowers to the sweet little girl. Diva was delighted with the respect she just had been given in front of everyone. And she could not resist the act.

Soon a heart shape black forest cake came and I still looked at the counter to put a stop to everything. I could not find the manager and I remained seated there as I was the show starter.

"TO LOVE WITH LOVE" it was written over it with the white cream.

Everyone kept looking at our table. I felt a little shy but I tried to remain as normal as I could.

As the last surprise one waiter came with the guitar in his hand and I was shocked as it was to be played by Gill and I only had to sing a little poem for her. The waiter stood next to me trying to hand me guitar and I was trying to escape the sight.

Diva kept looking silently at what was happening here. She was also in shock because of what I was doing.

"You want to play it Mani, then I would like to hear it"; said Diva surprisingly and her voice showed her curiosity about is going to happen next.

"I never knew you play Guitar"; continues Diva, excited.

It was the pleasant and most beautiful smile I could have ever had from Diva and I wanted that it should be there forever. For the smile, I took guitar in my hand, I was all helpless here but to my rescue suddenly someone came with another guitar in his hand for giving some base.

It was Gill I could not recognize him at the first sight as I did not expect him to come over there at this time.

I went close to him.

"Why did you come here when the plan was cancelled?" I whisper.

"I went to your room and your mate told me he saw you were going to the café and I just came to check what the lover boy is up to"; uttered Gill slowly while giving me a smile.

"There I came to know you had a fight and you then planned to take her for coffee"

"And as they say a lot can happen over coffee then why not you try yours" said Gill looking into my eyes.

"Yes" I nodded my head.

"And man one thing more, you have got the guts; you are holding an instrument which you hardly know how to hold"; whispered Gill, giving a mischievous smile.

"Look at me the way I am holding it and just give strokes like I will do and sing the song. I will manage everything"; said Gill.

"Ok"; I nodded him back.

Gill gave the base and then I too followed him with low strokes which were hardly audible. I slowed down the strokes more so that my guitars sound not disturbing the real player.

I started with the song: ***Gulabi Aaankehein*** and the melody of the song took every one over. The lights went dim and everyone started enjoying the show. And somehow I managed to rescue myself.

I acted like a lover boy with a smile and acting like playing the Guitar and singing the song which was very romantic. With applause all over in the coffee shop I ended my last note.

"Nice Mani"; said Diva from one side.

Then I made another move and said aloud that I would like to present 2 lines to Diva in front of everyone. I kneel down and Gill stood next to me.

"When it seems an end of this world I would like to make my start with you"

"This world is meaningful and its just coz I have you..."

"This life is worth being with you...a lot may come and go but..."

"Something I had for you and unspoken, unimaginable yet so simple like dew drops and so complicated like Newton's law."

"But thc law of lovc: don't havc cxplanations"

"No calculations and no derivations"

"It just crosses the barrier of Gravitational pull when it falls, the electromagnetic forces when it charges up"

"Now what to do when I am standing here in front to f you helpless waiting for your answer"

"Do I need a law of attraction here to get you?" I said as I look into Diva's eyes.

She seemed to be slightly unhappy.

"Sit down Mani I know this was great but I am not prepared for all this. Don't make a show here" said the girl angrily but yet in a convincing way.

She smiled back to all but her eyes asked me to stop and everything turned to its normal state while we had our cup of coffee as Gill left us in midst of our love story. With every sip I tried to search for an answer which was hidden into Diva's eyes. She could not lift her head and I could not get to it.

It only seemed so perfect but a question about our friendship was raised. It was now up to Diva whether to upgrade our friendship or let everything fall apart. While moving out I knew that things had not ended up well, so I moved on to my last act which was a card I wished to give her. Something I was writing for her to gift her from past many months and now it was time as my emotions for Diva were out in the open and I knew if it did not happen now it will never happen.

I held Diva's hand as she moved away from me and I pull her close to me. With the paper in my other hand…

"There's something I need to explain"; said Diva.

"Take it Diva. If you don't like it, don't keep it but at least read it once." I handed over a letter to her and turned to other side while Diva held it in her hands. She went home and read the letter which said:

The Propose...

Dear Diva,

There are some unspoken words
which I feel for you and want you to know
them and feel what I feel...
I want you to hear those unspoken things,
which is just like the taste of water,
things you feel but difficult to express
but can be told only when other feels.
It's just like being freshen up when you drink water
and that's what I feel after meeting you...
You have changed my life
just like water turns into ice
so keep this relation cool but don't
let this ice of relationship to melt...

With Luv,

Mani...

CHAPTER 5
BREAKUP

Meha was still around but in little contact with me. After the act and reading my poem as proposal, Diva got confused about her feelings for me and Kabir. Diva and Kabir were confused about their relationship; and it was the latest update from Karan. Karan told me the stud was out with some other gal when Diva caught him read handed and it became a problem in their smooth relationship. It was winning point and the best time for me to enter her life. I started my fancy with Diva. I started calling her every evening to ask her what she did for the whole day and this is how I got her engaged with me.

++Some wise words: When a girl is going through a break up, a shoulder to cry upon is the best thing for the one giving it and bad for the one for the one in relation.++

I was the one here giving a shoulder to Diva and Kabir was

the one in trouble.

Diva was coming close as I regularly started writing and gifting poems to her, talking each day. Every moment spent with Diva was fruitful. More I came close to her, better she came to know me.

++As it's wisely said: Some girls care about looks, some care about brains, but ALL girls want a guy who loves and cares for them++

I cared for her, expressing my love for her but what was lacking here was that I could not make her feel the same. I stopped calling Meha completely by this time and I was in no contact with her. Meha came to know about my affair with Diva from somewhere else. She called me up

Rings

"Is what I am hearing right?" said Meha, sounding disturbed.

She was disturbed from each side. First her sister was my class mate and now when she had a fight with her sister for me.

"I am sorry but I love Diva"; said I to Meha trying to console her for whatever I did to her. I knew I was the culprit but I was helpless too.

"And you are my classmate's sister"; I continue.

"Don't try to give it a political flavor"; said Meha in anger.

"What you are doing here with Diva as you say and what you did to me, what was that?" questioned Meha.

"Affection"; I reply slowly.

++ It is said: Affection is an infection and Love is a disease. For a healthy living you have to stay away from both++

"Don't confuse affection with the love"; I said justifying myself.

"Don't give lame excuses"; said Meha, very angrily.

"I know you are disappointed but please try to understand"; said I trying to end the conversation.

"Well what you want from Diva, you could have asked me"; said Meha to make me feel like I was interested in Diva sexually.

"It's not like what you are saying. I want nothing from her or you. But the thing is you are in love with me the same way I love Diva and from her side I don't know." said I.

"What about Diva then"; said Meha.

"I don't know..."

"What if she doesn't accept you?"

"Better make a choice now or else you will lose me as well"; said Meha.

"I think I would like to be with Diva rather than you Meha. I know you are a sweet girl but I am not as sweet as you. I might be a loser but I have to go to college and face your elder sister every day. And if I am not with Diva, I do not want to be with you either. Diva is just a part or a phase but I know this much and have decided to stay with her" I said all, trying to convince her but the talk took a bad end.

"You are playing with fire and you might burn your hands..."

Then she uttered some bad words and shed tears. I could help her but her words were inscribed deep on my mind that yes I was playing with fire which could burn my hands as well as my soul too. I decide not to call the two ladies to end up this confusion.

Before I decided to move out of Diva's life I made a last call to say goodbye.

Rings

"Ya Manav"; said Diva.

I was bit in a serious way and to the point I start the conversation with my feelings.

"Look Diva it is a mess where you are still in love with Kabir and me loving you."

"May be in this life time I won't get you but I would like to say: Is this my fault that Kabir enter yours life before I could enter?" said I expressing myself.

Diva kept me listening as I start proposing her unintentionally....

"And this thing will hurt me more in my life time that if I love someone so much, I am still unable to make her realize it"

"Is it so hard for the girls understand and always love someone who is not serious about them? Someone who could easily say cheesy lines to them and ignoring them who are true to their heart with no statements and cheesy lines. With just lame faces, dumb brains, and empty pockets but yet a true loving heart that beats for just a smile. A single gaze, as important as oxygen…"

"But the one who loves you, it is hard to say even the three words of love which I am unable to confess but the thing is that these are expression of love and not words sweetie"

"Why are you talking so differently"; said Diva.

I was still trying to say everything I had to and did not listen to her distractions.

"And if I am a loser here, I admit I am a loser and before I go out of your life I would like to give my best poem to you and after that I will be all gone."

Diva kept mum.

"I will drop the poem at your gate. Try to get it; I will make a call when I will"

And with this I ended the conversation. Later that afternoon I went to her house. Her house was not very far, I took my poem along with me and went to the gate of her house and dropped the poem inside. Then I ring her up to get it from there at the gate and went back home.

Lines of the poem were:

Poem: I still desire

I still desire for something which I cannot get,
I know, I have a hope while I cannot met,
That's why I like walking in the rain,
It doesn't show you my tear and my pain...
Whatever I have lost I pray you have gained,
I just like walking in the rain...

I can feel the wind and the rain drops,
They can help my tears but can't help them stop...
I still desire for something I cannot get,
In my hearts heart it's just love I felt,
You just can't help me and not my cry,
I know I am left lonely,
You are the one who is not giving a try...

Love u always
Mani...

CHAPTER 6

A NEW BEGINNING

Diva and me

Strange ***haina***... After so much of hard work, finally I convinced Diva to settle down and give a start to our relationship. It was decided between Diva and me that if anyone anytime wants to quit from this relationship they can, it was not compulsory that one has to give any appropriate reason for the back-off and friendship will remain there forever as it is. As we know beggars are not choosers so I gave a pleasant welcome to all the unethical conditions she put. And finally, Diva and I were very happily together now and it was a happy start after a broken heart. I was being a bit careful this time to my newly formed relationship. I started dating my dream girl and it was like a dream come true. For a safer date we decide her college to be the spot for the meetings. I started visiting her college regularly and chose her college balcony to meet almost every day and my studies started suffering. I stopped attending my college and started attending my love classes with Diva at her college. Things were going great between Diva and me. We both started making out outside the college too and started to go for long drives. We would drive together on her scooty as I hugged her from the rear seat while she drove all the way from one destination to other.

Time was going well together in a good way till her college tour. It was time when Diva was going out of the station for a whole month for the college tour and I knew I was going to miss her a lot.

Rings

"Mani I am going for a college tour and I know you would not like it but I really want to go out with my classmates and friends. It will be just for a month. So, I hope you will come and meet me. We will have only one chance and that is when my dad will drop me for the bus tomorrow morning "; said Diva all in a single breath as soon as I pick up the call as she was excited at the thought of going out for holidays.

I could not say anything more than saying yes will meet.

"Yes I'll come"; said I as I looked outside the window.

The mountains nearby were all snow capped. It was the winter season and the cold was at its extreme.

"Where are you exactly going?" I ask Diva further with a pause.

"It's a tour to Kanyakumari"; said Diva.

"And you are telling me now. This plan must have been fixed long ago"; said I as I wanted to make her feel special before she would leave but she told me the plan at the last point so I was helpless.

I always had this thought of gifting her flowers every time she would go somewhere out and came back, so it was a part of my routine for past few times. I looked at my watch it was late in the evening and flowers were not possible now. I knew I cannot get flowers at this late hour and at this season it was difficult to get flowers because of the cold. Still I decided to go to next station the very next moment to get the flowers, if there were any.

Plan was made within seconds and just needed to be followed. I really wanted that I might surprise Diva by not telling the concept as she herself knew I would not get the flowers this time of the season but I wanted my special thing to happen.

In next few hours after searching our place and a no from everywhere, I started my journey to the next town to get flowers for my girl. Karan went along with me, I kicked his bike to a start and he rode along with me went to the other town markets to search and get the flowers but I could not find any. Then I decided to get a gift for her. I was a bit sad because whatever I wished to have I was getting not even close to that. This was really a hectic time for me as Diva kept calling and I kept ignoring her all the time as I could not attend the call while driving and to keep my little secret. One the way back to my town, this time Karan was driving the bike and suddenly on the way we saw a house with a beautiful lawn. He slowed down the bike and both of us looked at its beauty.

"What do you say?" says Karan to me.

"What?" I reply back.

I knew what Karan was all about but I wanted to hear his idea so I gave him a very innocent look.

"Should we…" said Karan with a mischievous smile on his face.

"It's late in the evening, can we knock their door and do you think they will allow us to have these lovely roses"; said I.

"Do you think we are going to ask them up for your gift"; said Karan mischievously.

Karan slowed down the bike and put it on stand in the next lane. We both started walking towards the house, Diva was still calling me and at this time with nervousness I switched off my mobile. So this pissed off Diva a lot by it but I was going to rob someone's lawn to get flowers for my GF.

"So Karan who will go inside first"; said I.

"Of course you Romeo"; Karan replied back.

There was no way out so I climb up the wall and entered the house with an easy leap. I started plucking the flowers to make a bunch. While I was busy suddenly door opened and a lady came out shouting at me. Before I could find out what the situation is I ran out leaving the flowers behind. Karan kept on calling me from outside and in no time I was out of the house and we both ran near the place where bike was parked.

"What man! You threw the flowers; fuck you!" said Karan with a low feeling, hitting his fist on the wall.

"Fuck you idiot, you were there outside so as to give me a cover"; I reply back.

"And I was confused, that lady came suddenly shouting and she was screaming like anything"; trying to defend himself.

"Now what?" said Karan asking for our next move.

I waited for a second to gain control over my breathing.

"I really want those flowers, they are of no use to this owner lady"; said I sadly.

"Then what"; enquire Karan for my next move.

"I am going to talk to her"; said I while taking steps back to the situation we just ran out a moment ago.

Karan followed me while I started moving towards the house where I was just pointed at as a thief a minute ago. I stood in front of the gate of this big and lovely house but this time I was entering the house in a very gentlemanly way. I saw the lady standing in the porch of the house with a coffee mug in her hand. She looked wise and well educated.

Before entering the house, I took a look at the plate checking for the owner of the house.

"Bgr. Singh's Villa"

I stood in front of the gate and looked at the lady. I said to start the conversation.

"Hi. I know you think I am a thief and a vandal, but could you please hear me out for a moment" I said

"Well Mrs. Singh I wanna admit that I am in love with someone and love can make people do anything. All I was doing was wrong but I think this wrong is right when done in love, these flowers, I would have never plucked but I think I need them most."

"These were for my lady love"; I continued being, softly this time.

Still the lady didn't show any interest in what I was saying.

"Moreover I must say you and Mr. Singh; seems like you both had a love marriage so you can understand what I want to say…as you are a beautiful lady"; I knew that all female genes like some words like beautiful, cute to divert their attention.

"And Mr. Singh might have done even crazier things than this, stealing flowers from your garden and if I need them for my sake, I would not have given a second thought but it is for my Gf and I don't care about anything so I didn't looked back to ask you for them"; said I telling her that I am Romeo and not a gully guy.

"But you could have asked like a gentle man"; said Mrs. Singh this time a little pleased.

"I could have but it was too late in the evening to knock someone's door"; said I giving a convincing statement.

"I don't think you deserve these"; said lady pointing the flowers kept on the table and moving inside the room.

I could not think of anything other than having them.

I tried again; Karan kept telling me not to do such an idiotic thing. Love was on my mind and nothing could stop me.

I entered inside the house and I tried climbing the railing with some kind of vine tossed over it. I tried to grip one end of the bunch just kept near to the railing on the table kept close. On the first move as I slid my hand inside the railing I could not get a grasp to the bunch but in two or three tries I got my hand over it and as I had the flowers in the hand my other hand lost its grip to hold and with all the equations of gravitational laws I fell on the bed of grass into the garden. I could have my hands on the bunch now as they fell over me while my head touched the ground.

As I came to my senses I moved slowly and now the flowers were in my hand.

I move out of the house but something was still left undone and unproved. So I turned and went back.

"Stop Mani, are you a fool?" said Karan.

I went near the gate and pressed the bell of the house and went onto the road. Mrs. Singh came out of the house again. I point towards the bunch in my hand with a smile saying "Thank you"; while showing her the bunch and bowing a little.

"You won Romeo"; said Mrs. Singh with a smile and waving her hand.

"I was just checking you, was just wondering if you will dare to enter again or run back"; said Mrs. Singh showing her cunning intentions.

I too nodded my head, said" Do I deserve them now?"

"You deserve the girl too"; said Mrs. Singh.

"We don't have such Romeos now-a-days"; she continue.

Waving my hand at her I went back to my bike, Karan, who was watching the whole act was amused.

He kick started the bike and we drove back to our town.

Once I reached back, I put the flowers in the fridge and called Diva back.

No reply came from other side, Diva had switched off her mobile and the plan to meet her was also doubtful now. But it was decided nothing could stop me from meeting her now. So I decided to go out early in the morning and stand in front of her door and would watch her going out for the bus and would follow her all the way till I get a chance to talk to her.

But God had something else to show, very next morning it started raining and it was very cold outside.

But Love was running through my veins and nothing could have stopped me at that moment, I decided to go out on my scooter as I had to go out early in the morning without disturbing my father so getting car out of garage would disturb dad's dreams and my dream to meet Diva too.

I get onto my scooter and went to stand outside her home; there was no place to stand other than standing in the rain. I kept standing there for half an hour till I saw her room's light from the window. This light from her room gave me courage to be there for the next one hour. I was all wet in the rain, cold, shivering and my eyes they could hardly blink. I could not even feel my lower half but love was giving me strength to stand there. Diva being unaware of the fact that I was standing outside her home, went with her father in the car without noticing me. I kick my ride and tried to reach the spot where she was going to catch her bus for the trip. I followed her all the way and I could not feel anything other than severe cold.

Her father kept on talking to her on the way and I stood near the tree hiding myself just to see when her father will go out of the sight and I will get a chance to meet her.

Nothing happened as I had planned and finally the bus left for the journey and I could not met Diva and neither could I give her the flowers.

I came back home and for the whole next month Diva didn't speak to me and I knew she was angry because of my ignorance.

I still find the reasons how could she forget to call me in the end and I still knew why but I was assured that when she comes back I will be there under the tree waiting for her after a month.

And finally after a month, Diva came back.

I stood there under the same tree waiting for her. Her father was again there this time and I was standing with those flowers wrapped in the paper properly. I knew they were all dry but yet they were special. Diva still preferred not talking to me so I called her up.

Rings

"Hey diva"; said I.

"What do you want Mani" reply Diva in anger.

"I don't think you have time for me"; she continue.

"It's not like that"; I tried to defend myself.

"Yes it is and its true, I tried to call you all the time to give you time to meet me and you being so rude to me, to this relationship and this all is so casual to you. If you are really uninterested then you can clear yourself out and we will make a deal that we will never see each other again. At least it will be less hurting"; Diva just blew up with her anger.

"Hey I was there"; said I.

"Where...? And don't you try to fool me Mani"; said Diva but this time her pitch was rather low.

"Near to the tree as I am now"; said I.

"I have something for you. If we are still in relation can we meet somewhere"; said I again.

"Come inside the bus I will be there but for two minutes because Dad is here dropping my luggage in the car so we don't have ample of time"; said Diva seems pleased.

I went inside the bus get a hold of my darling from her waist close to me, other girls kept looking me. Diva kept ignoring me and tried her level best to show her anger to me. She threw my hand from her waist. As I had travelled all the way with all these daring acts, it was time to show a little more of me to Diva.

I held her hand tight this time and sat on the seat whereas Diva tried to escape.

"You are hurting me Mani"; said Diva in pain.

"So do you when you ignore me but the difference is that men don't show they cry and when they cry, they cry from their heart"; I said to her, in pain.

Diva looks into my eyes as I say harsh words to her.

Her eyes were wet not with the pain. She knew what pain I was going through when she was ignoring me. She too wanted to talk to me but her ego didn't let her to talk.

++Some wise words: Anger may kill the relation, misunderstandings may kill people but ego kills all+++

Still in ego she took the gift and said nothing and moved ahead.

She said" I will call you"; while getting out of the bus.

I waited there till she left with her dad, sitting alone and thinking why I tried to hurt her.

But I could not find any answer. I went back home. I was relieved at least now those flowers were with their real owner.

In the evening Diva rang me up. She was a little numb this time she had lay go of her ego when she saw the flowers and came to know that I was there standing waiting for her. All these misunderstandings we had put us into no contact for a whole month. This hurt her and so she asked me to meet as soon as I could manage. I too wanted to spend some quality time with her so we decided to make out some day.

Diva said sorry for all the things that happened unintentionally. Finally at our meeting I told her the whole incident about how I managed to get those flowers and how special they are to me. Hearing the entire daring act Diva promised she will never let this relationship down. But my happiness could not stand as Diva had met Kabir on the tour. It was heart breaking news for me as I was doing so much for my girl and she was betraying me but I kept mum.

++It is well said: A girl's ex will always be in her memory, but the guy she loves now will stay in her heart++

I just ignored it and never asked Diva for that. It was my trust for her and I forgot the fact in a day or two. Life went on as smooth as it could.

With the flowers the poem, which I gifted, was:

Poem: "11 roses and a fake one"

I said that I will love you
till the last one dies
Coz I don't want to lose you...

Now I look back and say the same,
I always smile to hide my pain,
Don't forget me may be I was bad,
Don't lose what we had,
Now whatever happens,
I will never forget...

I think of you and I cry,
Why you say that and never gave a try..

When I thought to say you last good bye,
I really wanted to give you something special...
Don't know what, when and why

I look for everything till the end,
When I finally decided to give you
"11 roses and a fake one"...

I never thought to lose you...

And I say again "I love you"

CHAPTER 7

TRUE LOVE

What is true love? Someone asked and it was hard to define. Something inexpressible and which can really be felt when the person whom you love is missing from your life. It is something you cannot replace.

++Someone asks: Where does love got its origin from? And its reply was China. If it don't have to replenish it might not work till evening and if it has to work it might work for years++

And I always ask myself why stories about love are hard. Examples given are for those who could only get their love but could not live with love... Romio Juliet, Heer Ranjjha, ME and Diva... We all were in the same category now.

I came to know about it when Diva was gone out of my life. Someone I missed so badly and I wanted to be with her but then suddenly spending a day or two together with a final decision that we are no one to each other now and together, there is no future. We end this relation there.

Mistakes which were overlooked are now looked as a reason not to be together. This is true love when you accept the one as it is. I came to know about the one I love when I was no longer with her and when I was forced to live alone at the time when I wanted to live with her the most.

++Someone has said: After LOVE if there's something else to happiness then let me know. I want to hear that… ++

Incidents happened as:

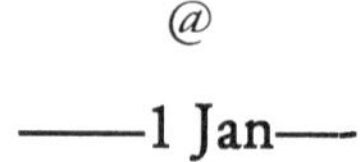

——1 Jan——

Everyone was celebrating New Year and so was I. This year was different from the rest of the years; I had a resolution in the mind for the year. I called Diva up.

Ring.

And in a ring or two I was connected to Diva.

"Hello"; said I in a very romantic way this time.

"Hi! Happy New Year sweetie"; reply Diva with the same attitude and a telephonic kiss.

<Confused: Well an e-kiss or a telephonic kiss is just an expression of kiss, a sound or a XOXO for the love over electronic media>

"Well I have a confession to make"; said I.

"Pretty nice to hear, hope not a big one"; reply Diva in a loving way.

"I don't ever want to hurt you knowingly or unknowingly. I hope you will keep me updated that I am good with you. If I ever go slow just hold my hand and give me support to love you…"

"Call me if I ever forget to, meet me if I ever forget to and do slap me if I ever forget to pat you, coz I love you"

"I just want to say I will always keep you happy and will never give you a single chance that you will say: Hey Mani is bad, he doesn't care about me"; said I and my eyes got wet.

So were Diva's at the other side I could judge it from her breaths.

"Why do you always do this Mani" said diva in a crying manner.

"What did I do now? I Want to keep you happy always"; said I.

"I wanna meet you Mani"; said Diva. "Sure" said I confidently.

And the conversation ended soon with some love quotes and me crying along with Diva with her words that" I feel I am not up to mark to you and I still wonder why you are with me"

"And I hope you will stay with me always and forever"; said Diva dropping the call.

I tried her number many times but it was switched off. May be my words were too harsh for her and she was into something I never knew. I really never knew her nor her feelings. I just got to know this when we broke up.

Her messages kept on beeping "I will never let this relation down from my side and I hope you also do the same".

I stored each and every message of her in separate folder of my mobile and used to read and cry for a while. Then finally I made a decision to make her feel really special this time.

In the meanwhile Diva's father got transferred to another place so she joined another college then after and took a PG.

@

—19 Jan—-

A thought with one dream to make her feel special kept moving in my mind all the time and I was not even prepared nor did I have any idea how to execute it till I had a dream of "21-Cards". It was her birthday and I wanted to make her feel special before I met her on Valentine's Day.

I started preparing for it, I went to each shop pick up cards of my choice- the most adorable and selected ones; so that I could make a bunch of cards of my choice and this thing continued till I searched 21 cards in my hand. But still something was missing, so I decided to put a love letter in each card signifying every year of her birthday with a hand written love note with my thoughts to tell her what would be my feelings if I would have been there in her life long before and what would I have done special for her on the b'day I missed.

I did a full-fledged survey for it. I went to her school, gathered information about her and talked to her sister about it so that the thing should remain real close to her life. Finally the day came when I posted each and every card written each year on it signifying my love for her that I could not make to her in all these years when I was missing out of her life.

On the day when she got the card, I got a call from Diva.

Ring

"I want to read all these cards with you Mani"; said Diva crying.

"Hey Diva c'mon these all are for you, it will take a whole day in travelling for me to reach "; I reply back.

"No I want you here with me"; said Diva and her words were very straight.

"Okie"; I promise to meet as I put down the line.

++Lover's book ***funda*** no. 56: You can win from a girl but cannot win from a girl when she's crying, knowingly or unknowingly…++

Finally I made a plan, in few days I went to make out with her and travel all the way to her place to read cards with her and I still knew what I had written in that but to make her feel special I had no choice.

@

—29 Jan—

I went to Diva's room. All things were at their place like a typical girlish room whereas a boy's room would look like a store. Only one thing which was noticeably different here was her green colored room rather than pink one but still it was awesome. She was PG at someone's place but it never seems to as the place was friendlier.

We were alone and it was romantic. Diva cooked something for me which she called her own prepared recipe but looked like a ***masala maggi***. It was special and it was real, it was something unforgettable. Diva opened her cupboard and dropped all the cards which I gave her on the bed.

"So from where should we start?" said Diva, with a smile, looking into my eyes.

My girl was looking as beautiful as ever in the best fitted long white skirt and a scarf with a sky blue top. I could not resist throwing some cheesy lines.

"From kissing to the foreplay"; said I looking at her eyes passionately.

"No Mani be serious I am talking about cards"; said Diva pointing towards the cards.

I took one of the red envelopes and Diva sat next to me while I started reading the card. Then I gave her the task to choose which ever card she likes and I read the card for her explaining what I felt when I wrote the particular card. After an hour or so I asked Diva to give me her comments for the very best lines she read from all the cards.

"Diva which one would you say, is most touching line to you?" I ask.

"The one saying, I want to be at the very next desk on the school when you first started using your first Ink pen and I would love to see marks of those inks on you face while I study along with you each day looking at you innocently."

"Sometimes I would borrow notebooks from you and sometime you would borrow a pen"

"And in this way our whole would life just surround each other"

Her words had a true feeling and a tear of innocence.

"Which one is your favorite Mani?" asks Diva searching for love in my eyes and my eyes welled up.

"The favorite one is still in my heart and not in these cards Diva"; said I while crying from inside.

Diva looked into my eyes and asks "Which one? I want to know…"

Looking into her eyes and being silent for some time:

"I want to have a baby girl after our marriage and I want to name her Diva" said I.

"Why?" this much only came from Diva's mouth opened.

"Because this is how I will have 2 Diva's in my life"; I said while maintaining the eye contact.

"The two lovely ladies of my life…" I continued and a tear rolled down my cheek.

Listening to this, Diva could not react to anything other than covering me with her arms. We hugged together for a while and then

I make a move. I kiss her on her neck which she always say's it cares her a lot. Then I kiss her on her lips while looking into each other's eyes. It was a memorable sight. Diva was into my arms and we were in a lip lock. I made another brave move and slid my hand into her top for which she did not react and just kept looking into my eyes with a sigh of agreement. I kissed her lips again, onto her neck and all the way I kissed her ears. While I kiss her on her ears I would whisper little "Love you" into her ears and she could only moan to it as a reply. I moved more and we lay on the bed looking into each other's eye to see love. The thing went on for around 20 minutes and we could hardly remember anything, till the bell from microwave distracted us. Then we had our lunch together and I came back to my friend's place which was in the same city. Before moving out Diva gave me her sky blue scarf as a token of love from her side for the first physical touch.

"Hope you keep it with you forever"; says Diva while roping me with the scarf and pulling me over it.

"Definitely"; said I looking at her.

I came close and kissed her lips again while holding her head with my hands. And Diva click the pic of this special moment with her mobile while I kissed her pink lips.

"Am I gonna have this pic"; I ask for the pic while moving out of the building.

"Do check your mail for it"; says Diva for the pic. I took an auto rickshaw and moved back.

Diva kept messaging me all the way saying thanks and love for the special day.

@

—4 Feb—-

I was about to go back to my place happily but I felt something fishy. All was in place till the spy friend of mine decided to be the killjoy. Yes Karan. The one who always made my life hell with his news was once again there in my life in with something.

++ Some wise words: Something is necessary not to be known for the betterment than knowing them unknowingly++

But God had something else to show me. Karan gave me new idea to hack social website as he was doing ethical hacking course. I had no one to do this and no one on whom to do this.

"You should give a try"; said Karan on telephone.

"To whom"; I reply.

Karan wanted to show his basics over the ethical issue but I was not that much social to have an account to social networking website.

"I am mailing this little program on your email"; said Karan like he had won this world with his skills.

I downloaded the software on my friend's desktop and it remained there for sometime but always searching for mischief's I could hardly control myself to give a pain to someone. Finally with a fair mind set

I decided to give Diva a tension of hacked e-mail address, so for social service, I decided to hack Divas profile once. I opened Karan's hacking project and enter social service with Diva's ID and open her ID in a minute with this software.

But to surprise Diva was rather tough than surprising myself with her Inbox indicating messages beeping. I never wanted to spy her so I close the account and lay down but in few hours I could not resist checking those emails. I opened the hacking software again and her account. I clicked the mail icon on the top and I could not believe myself. Her Inbox was full of her ex-boy friend's messages – Kabir, was back again.

Yes! The Inbox was filled with Kabir's messages and I could hardly believe myself.

I got an ache in my stomach and I vomited at the same time. Something so bad happened to me and it was something so painful like someone was peeling out my skin and killing me slowly. It was worse than taking my life away.

I read all the messages Diva and Kabir had exchanged. Some were so heart breaking where Kabir asked her that whether she is with the same guy referring me or she had changed her boy friend during these years.

To the reply Diva answered Kabir that she is alone all the way after Kabir left her and Mani could never took his place. I cried a lot and I was all broken after these messages. It was something not to be shared and to be discussed to anyone. I had no one to share all this with and I hated Diva for doing this to me.

++ Someone had said: If you scratch my back I will scratch yours++

I was still confused to it that I am scratching her back then who is scratching mine. It was more than stabbing. I swallowed this thought for Kabir to tell him that what is happening to my life and decide not to go back. I read the last message, the one saying that two are going to meet somewhere soon when I will travel back home.

I was all broken but I decide to face the situation like a man. Keeping an eye on her emails further, I came to know the finalized dates between them and it was 14-feb. After me meeting Diva she was planned to have another date and I thought myself to be cheated as the girl called me earlier all because she wanted to meet her Ex boy friend next. Great…

When I confronted her she said she doesn't love him anymore and did not admit anything about Kabir. Her only thing she admits was she will meet the guy if by chance she will come across Kabir and that will only be a casual meet nothing special. I gave a positive attitude to it as I knew the two will meet even if I also say no to it. I lie Diva about my plan going back to my place back for some urgent work but I remain there to see the whole thing with my eyes as I was still not believing what I read on mail. I never had an idea that something like this could ever happen to me and I still find myself in a night mere that will end soon.

@

—14 Feb—-

Finally the day came and I was here at her city to see everything through my eyes. I took a bunch of roses for the girl and dressed up as I used to meet her. I went to the place where they both decided to meet. I enter the decided hotel. It was near to her PG. I took seat from where I could see whole of the space but can hide myself. I order soda for myself and start waiting for the love birds. Unaware of my presence, Diva and Kabir enter the restaurant in a very close fashion. Kabir's hand was on Diva's waist. They look too much intimate. I could not hold the sight but it was the truth in the end of the day I had to face. I react very normally keeping a stone to my heart and stabilizing my outburst of emotion here. I try to look more to their act. They both took their seat. Diva was wearing something flaunting her beauty to get an appreciation from her ex. Her top was short and was rather revealing, I could see how everyone in the restaurant noticing her. It was sure that under Kabir's influence this girl was acting so plastic to impress him again. I always knew Kabir was stud and Diva could do anything to impress him as he was the first love of her life. It was not easy for Diva to forget him. I tried my best to overcome Kabir but helplessly now the results were in front of my eyes. Kabir asked the waiter to take the order and while placing the order both of them held hands and look into each other's eyes. Kabir was saying something to Diva and Diva kept smiling at Kabir's compliment with a blush and the smile. I could feel how happy they were together then where do I stand in her life. I could see Kabir's foot rubbing against Diva's leg. Rest I could not dare to see so I tried not to look there. My heart was numb and I could not react there. I wanted to go and slap her just there in front of everyone but I knew for the past few months I was playing with the fire. My hands had to get burnt. I left Meha for her and this was something Meha warned me of. I did not believe anyone when I was told that the two of them met at times like the time when Diva had gone to the tour and now I was watching the entire thing there. I was helpless so I decided to go back home empty handed. It was hurting and I did not want to face Diva coz my trust was broken. I went back without saying anything. Before leaving the place I tried to take a last look at her. I saw what I never wanted to. The two kissed each other and as their lips touched, a tear rolled down my eyes. I was crying from my heart and eyes were just reacting to my heart. I had these roses for the girl. I knew I am not gonna meet her but I always used to give her flowers when we meet. So how come not today when I am here I am not giving her roses? I call upon the waiter while the two were happily enjoying their date. I gave the bouquet to the waiter and a tip of 100 bucks to give the flowers to her and they had a last note with them. I switched off my mobile and went out of the restaurant crying hard.

I thanked God that day it rained so heavily that my tears got wiped away with the raindrops. The clothes I was wearing got all wet but the cigarette still lit and with two puffs taken from it, like my GF it also left me in midst. I sat near the road thinking about my value in her life; for hours and with my head on my hands I looked upon the sky.

"I will never come back..." came from my mouth as I stood up and went towards my friend's apartment and the truth of a silent breakup remained buried in my heart.

The letter which I gave to her that day along with the roses:

LAST LETTER

Dear

Diva,

It's not like I am asking you to love me but there's something in my heart and it's just a hope

I still dream to hold your hand and I knew it will hurt me more not you if I am thinking about you but I will keep my feeling shining as always

and I promise I will not give you any look that will remind you of me and the older times when you look at me just to see the pain I am having since you left me... it's still there

Anything can be understood with closed eyes and silent lips but the words that hurts me more is your words asking me "not to love you.."

when I know I can't help myself loving you and that not be for even single second of a day...

All I can say now that I am sorry I cannot love you with these conditions coz its hurting... and I am hurt...

Forgive and forget

Love you always,

MANAV.

CHAPTER 8
BREAKUP AND IT HAPPENS AGAIN

I don't know how many breakups a person can overcome but I was just adding one with each try. Leaving Diva's city, on the way, I was so much depressed with what happened to me. I knew I was a loser. Diva had nothing to lose. She had a pure heart that only beats for Kabir and I was the one for whom she never cared about. But still there was a hope from inside in my heart that one day she will come back to me but this spark was dying and I realize that somehow I have to start a new life again without Diva.

While I was in the sea of tears, Krishna came to my room. I was all sad lying on my bed.

Looking at me with a big "O" on his face, the only thing that came from Krishna's mouth was:

"What the fuck!!!"

"What have you done with yourself"; Said Krishna looking at my uncombed hair and unshaven beard.

"Are you into some kind of depression or what?" continued Krishna.

Well Krishna was one of my fast friends, also my neighbor at the hostel. We share a common balcony as well as share some common thoughts. It was a hard time when I met Krishna last time when I was going through my first break up and at the same time he was also suffering from the girlfriend disease so dealing with the common diagnosis and taking the same treatment. But it was a time when Krishna and I used to share a world of **Poly-girlfriend-ia** (many Gf's at a time) but now things were changed for me. I changed my self for the girl who changed my life into hell.

"What a mess have you made with your life, c'mon move from this dirty place and come to my room. I have this new latest Walker wine lets share it while we look into your matter"; said Krishna bossily like my elder brother and this was something I needed most.

Without wasting time I went along with Krishna to his room.

With the matchstick lit and the cigarette lightened up before Krishna turned on the light of his room. On entering I could see the forehead lines of Krishna as if he was worried about me.

Handling his cigarette to me and giving me a dirty look as if I had made such a big blunder. By the time I haven't said anything but his eyes bore deep into my thought.

"What??" that only I spoke the moment Krishna re-entered the room.

“Nothing man just have a look at this thing”; Krishna with a smile pointed out the bottle kept on the table.

“I was thinking of a party tonight but I think we need to discuss the matter tonight and this thing will goes down in the gut and the words will come out”; said Krishna.

This is how we do it, man to man always, Krishna knew my style.

“Hm…” this only I could say as the sign of my agreement and taking the last puff of the cigarette. By the time he was searching for the glasses and talking, I smoked 2 cigarettes.

Table was set and all things and the toxicant were kept with the peanuts. The man-to-man talk started all the way which was going to take place all night till the last drop ends.

“I am fucked again”; said I, yes I was, I was in love.

“C’mon tell me how I can help you, look Diva is your past and you have to go for someone to forget her” said Krishna.

I knew it will be a very helpful technique to divert my mind from Diva. But I need someone I really like. The thought of Gauri, my senior struck my mind. She was my first crush at college when I enter the hell. And again, this time Gauri was the one and I was confused.

“Gauri” I confess to Krishna.

“If you want to help me help me for her” said I.

Krishna kept looking into my eyes and then promised me to help me with Gauri.

Very next day, to help me out of my problems Krishna being my senior and a good friend of Gauri, talk to her and told her what I feel for her and ask her to help me out with the mental break down for Diva.

Gauri agree to help me out but with just friendship. We started to spend time together. I could tell Gauri everything about my life whatever was happening. We shared our numbers and with little effort and some expenses on message pack, eventually Gauri became a very good friend of mine.

We start our little friendship raised up from senior-junior relationship by messaging each other all night long.

———Life @ Hostel———

At 7 p.m, another day of my breakup party. I organize all- expense-booze party at my room. It was hard to get alcohol in hostel and to carry bulky beer bottles inside the premises. I came to the gate; there was standing Rajji bhaiya. I exchange the money with the bag full of the bottles and three ice filled packets kept in-between the bottles so that while walking they don't make any sound. I came to my room and call my buddies up. I took the bottle opener and kept everything from the peanuts to the box of ice on the study table.

Rahul and Monty two other drinker friends of mine joined the team where as Krishna also join the party but he was not very fond of partying and alcohol.

I put some Kishore Da's soft music and dim the light where as Krishna did not join the party but preferred staying there in the room just to accompany us for the drinks with his packet of cigarette. We started drinking the beer. I was not much into drinking and had just started to drink heavily.

Rahul said while taking the sip.

"Abhi this beer is not a man's stuff why don't we have something else next time"

"What??" I enquired.

"The real alcohol"; answers Monty.

"No" I reply back again.

"Yeas c'mon this is like a breezier a lady's drink"

"Let's taste the real thing"; said Monty again.

I looked at Krishna and he gave me a weird look and I had to flip the topic.

I said; "next time we will see. We will think over it" And the drinks were in and soon everything became blurred and I fell asleep.

@

Rahul & Monty an Old Story

These things started long before. It was first day of my college and the very day when problems with Rahul and Monty started. I was the culprit and I admit it. To continue my mischiefs and to add upon to my troubles, I together with Bhanu another friend of mine, made a plot for the two guys.

As they were boozing in the ***tapri*** (a place to fag); I made a plot there only.

"Hi how are you?" ask I to make a perfect start and to get myself attention.

Rahul look at me as I made a statement here and interfering in the midst.

"I just heard you people talking there that you two are also taking admission to the college"; continue I.

"So what, did you meet any seniors?" said I.

"No, not actually new to the college it's our first day in the college"; said the two simultaneously justifying themselves.

"Well me too. I am afraid of ragging"; said I allowing my cunning intensions to flood down from my words.

"Me to"; said Monty.

"OK"; I nodded with a reply.

As per the plan I gave a signal to Bhanu to enter into the situation.

"So 1st year"; said Bhanu.

"Yes who are you?" I enquire.

Bhanu made a grasp of my hair in his hand and pulls them hard to look into my eyes; "I am your senior and you all better meet me at the hostel."

This thing was enough to scare Rahul and Monty.

"You are going to repent now for this act"; said Bhanu signaling towards the cigarette lit on my hand.

As in front of the senior we were smoking and sitting on the place where juniors were not allowed to enter. The two came running towards Bhanu and tried to shake hands before things turned from bad to worse.

"We hardly know him"; said Monty to Bhanu.

"Don't try to fool me! You all were sitting together and making puffs. That's what I saw"; reply Bhanu, with a damn to both, as decided.

"Meet me at hostel"; said Bhanu commandingly pointing towards the yellow building.

"Sorry sir"; said Monty and Rahul again and again but nothing helped them.

Bhanu moved towards the college ground where as I followed with the two guys who were just in trauma of something they could not understand. I followed them till I got close.

"Which room"; said I asking Rahul and Monty while walking along.

"You better stay away from us"; said Monty making an attempt to make slow their cadence so that I could maintain a proper distance to them.

"C'mon' we together have to solve it otherwise as you wish…" said I.

"What next"; said Monty.

"Mine room is 344 and yours"; said I giving them a hint.

"305"

"Let's talk there only"; I suggest.

And we all went towards their room.

I took out my mobile and typed 305 and messaged Bhanu. Bhanu understood what I meant by numbers at the moment.

While we all settled down in the room Bhanu enters the room with a blow of the fist to the door. As with a loud voice to the door made us all stand instinctively and look at the door.

"Well you"; pointing towards me.

"Sorry sir"; said I.

"Come here I want to see you how you smoke"; said Bhanu with a cigarette in his hand.

"You both, you were also smoking"; said Bhanu adding to his ridiculous acting.

"No"; said Rahul fearfully.

"They were" I said accusing them along with me.

"He's lying"; said Rahul defending himself and taking few steps towards me so to add some weight to his point.

And yes I was lying they were innocent but in the plan they had to fit.

"You better make a puff throwing a matchbox on my face"; said Bhanu.

I pick up the box and started boozing up while Monty and Rahul looked at me from one corner.

"Hand it to the other two bastards too"; said Bhanu looking at them.

I offer cigarette to Rahul and Monty. They had no choice but to light the tobacco and make puffs.

"How long have you been smoking "; questioned Bhanu.

"2 years"; I said before anyone could answer.

"And you"; said Bhanu looking at Monty.

"I don't smoke at all"; reply Monty.

"Me neither" said Rahul in advance.

"I don't like liars I will make you run naked in the campus if I smell any lie in your answers"; said Bhanu angrily.

"I only drink"; said Rahul making a confession.

"Everyday?" asks Bhanu

"Occasionally"; reply Rahul.

Monty and I stepped back a little. Monty gave me a look as if he was very scared. I took gave him the same but I knew.

"How occasionally"

"You drink on occasions in front of your father"; said Bhanu.

I gave a look to Bhanu to stop him and his bad acting. But the boy was high with morale and continued his dirty dialogues altogether.

"No sir I mean I drink but not like this"; reply Rahul to Bhanu's question while me and Monty kept mum.

"How often your occasion... is"

"When we are happy"

"Aren't you happy you got admission here in this prestigious college" said Bhanu.

"Yes I am happy"; said Monty but in low pitch.

"Should we drink then?" said Bhanu and it was something undecided.

"Yes sir if you don't mind"; said Rahul taking all the charge of the party from the Monty and me.

With an agreement the two went out to buy drinks and made them ready for us by the evening and we could not stop laughing once they left.

@

— That night 10 pm—-

Room was all well prepared for a *masti* party by our two *bakras*. With sound of the opener we opened the beer bottles; I slid down the bottle to Monty. And then it was the time for the real tonic to open. The guys had the Rum arranged for us. None of us was so good in this flush drink.

Being seniors in eyes of the two we opened and made our pegs where as Rahul placed the chicken on the table.

"So where are you from?" asks Bhanu while taking his sip which looked like a black poison.

His drink was hard; Bhanu was a drinker from his schooldays. He was a known unsocial school rich delinquent child. I was still new to it.

"From JJSP School"; said Rahul with his collars up.

"So from a prestigious school of this country"; said Bhanu.

"Yeah"

"And you Monty"; this time in curiosity I question Monty.

"Same School"

"And you are taking this fluid which we call as pee, man just keep at least some reputation for the school"; Bhanu insult them again.

This was enough for the idiots to drop their beer bottle and mixing their drink with a large peg of Rum. This was what we call suicide. Loll...

For around 2 hours the party was on and we talked about everything from studies to gals. Then it was time to break the party so thanking the two we came out of their room laughing silently.

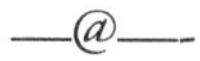

Other day at 8:30 am: first lecture

While most of the students leaning on their benches for quenching their thirst for sleep. I and Bhanu had our usual back seat. The class was big enough for us to cover our hangover whereas most of the students were busy with their introduction. I and Bhanu on the back bench were trying to open our eyes as we were not used to Rum.

As soon as everyone could settle down on their seats, suddenly all rushed to have a seat as it seems like our first teacher had entered the class.

Every one took the seat nearby. I and Bhanu keep mum to the whole scene and enjoy the studious chap of the college fighting for the front seat.

"For your roll call'; said the professor with harsh words and duster in his hand.

He started rubbing the board which was already new, with nothing written on it except for date. It seems like he was used to this entire act as he had been repeating it for years.

With the pen in his hand and dropping the duster there on the table the professor took his chair.

"Arshit"; with the first name he started looking into the attendance register.

Everyone started following their roll call and then suddenly when I attended my roll call; so Bhanu, as his roll call was next to me. I could hear some ugly words for us from the corner of the silent room.

"Bastard"; said Monty from one side with his eyes following his anger distracting Rahul from his book with his elbow blow. Rahul look at me with a shock. Rahul could hardly think for the prank where as Monty seems to be in revengeful attitude. His face was red and I knew he was very angry with me for all the drama but who cares we had the fun.

CHAPTER 9
WHAT IF

After my second breakup, I was so desperate to be in a relationship that I tried forcing myself to love someone but I could never find anyone who touched my heart. While some bad things happened to my life but still there were some more storms yet to hit me.

She was my teacher on whom I always had a deep crush. She was one of the beautiful bitches around the college. She was what every man wants. Whenever she used to come in the college with her tight pants would reveal her thighs and her little upper curves. I was one of the students who were very fond of thinking about her, watching her in the class all way attending and sitting in front of her, something I was doing from very first day of the college. She was the most beautiful and adorable woman on the campus.

It was the day when the sun was burning high and I was really not up to the mood of the class. As I was still hurting from the breakup but still I could make some time for my adorable eye tonic teacher. She was the one I talked mostly to, in my dreams and she could give me relief all the way. She was a perfect teaser like a playboy model.

Sometimes looking at her I used to put my head on my palms and could think of her in her lingerie and fantasize about her as a pole dancer and imagine her in the pose I wished for her. I could think of anything from doggy to any style on her. All this gives me extreme excitement in my blood and pants too. At least for that time I could feel relaxed and diverted from the break up melodrama and it was perfect to distract myself.

One day the situation was really erotic as she was in a sari and it was the first time I saw her in her backless sari. This was something new to me and of course all of us guys attending her class. I was slightly uncontrollable sitting on the first seat of the class. I always managed to sit on the first bench so that from there I could had a good view of her and her deep cleavage. She moved her hand combing her hair with her fingers while she moved from one line to other and I could note every moment of her till her eyes met mine. Sometimes from her attitude she signaled me that she has seen me watching her but who cares as long as I was getting my eye tonic. I wrote on my note book some lizzy words for her and then rubbed them out it. Today was the day the things were little more uncontrollable so I decide to go to toilet before I blew up because of my fantasies to distract myself. My man ship was hard so I decided to move.

"May I go to toilet"; I utter suddenly without thinking about the subject and standing up while I said for it.

She gave a strange smile, look into my eyes and my pants all together at the same time as if she was confused how can I say such a weird thing in the midst of the class while she on the most important topic of the subject.

Without any argument she agreed nodding her head and a little smile "yes sure".

And I without looking back went out the class to pee. But instead of going to toilet I went out to the canteen to distract myself. I took water and stood up there till I came out of my thought of her being seduced by me anyhow I could. I look at my watch and it was all late to attend the lecture further. So I decide not to go into the class and rather going back I decide to go the library and sit under in the air conditioned room. I went to library to cool myself but her thoughts still haunts my mind and I sat there keeping my head on my arms folding. I stood there for the next half an hour and fell asleep.

——Life @ Hostel——

At the usual hook ups at the hostel premises, it was now casual to see me at the so called hostel ***Daru party*** and I was one of the executive members of such parties. Life has changed a lot and so have I. Cigarette and alcohol were my best friends now and it was all I needed these days.

Liquor was on the table and the other executive members – Rahul and Monty at other side. Making 90-90 for the bottom up, we had a daru ego problem here.

"I was the one who used to have a whole bottle at my times when I was at boarding school Shimla'; said Rahul in his casual, self centered manner, at this time it was well nourished by the toxicant.

"Really I never saw you consuming that much"; I replied to him with a witty smile and with an "I don't care"- attitude.

This was hurting for his ego. He started again.

"Well I always had till last man stands to drink with me and by the way Manav you are still a kid so don't think you can stand in front of me"; said Rahul in a challenging way.

While saying this he took his mobile and SMSed something.

Krishna could see everything sitting there, while Monty too, was hung up with his mobile. The two were having a chat conversation which Krishna could smell easily.

Beep

My mobile beeps for SMS from Krishna. I took my mobile out and looked at the message

"Don't get into a fight"

I close the message.

And the conversation starts again, but this time with Monty.

"Why don't we have a bet on it."; said Monty in a convincing way, with Rahul nodding his head and to make a start he took the bottle in his hand.

"So what's the deal"; said Rahul.

I look at Krishna he was talking with his eyes and saying don't do anything foolish. But I was not in my senses and was ignoring him all the way. Krishna's attitude boosts me up more.

"What do we have to do?" I ask.

"Nothing much let's consume 90-90ml and it will be a last man standing and no puking "; said Monty.

"What's the deal in it, for the winner"; said Krishna trying to make it a bet on money so that I step aside if it is a big amount.

"Money"; said Rahul.

"No"; said Monty, "it is a matter of self respect"; he continued.

He wanted me to participate in the bet and he knew my pockets were empty and they will not find any ATM at this time so he changes the thing in a minute.

"Then for what?" I asked, confused.

"Well anyone has a 10 rupees currency here"; said Monty.

I took out the one I had in my pocket and said while showing it; "Yes here it is".

I throw it straight between us.

"That's it"; said Monty picking it up and with his pen he wrote something on it.

"For the one who stands his words"

That's from my side and passing pen to Krishna Monty said;"Now you write something on it"

In the honor of a drunken bastard... wrote Krishna... Now he was into the game and Rahul made a 90-90ml in two glasses.

"Pick it up Manav or do you want to quit'; said Rahul taunting me.

I looked at Krishna this time he gave me an agreement. I pick up my glass and with the click of the glasses held in our hands we start the bet. The 90 ml was in and a deep pain, a burning sensation hit my gut.

"Your turn my friend"; said I to Rahul while Monty looked sad.

He too had his ml in a second and with a dirty expression like his stomach was hurting a lot.

So the party was on with a bet and in 10 minutes we shared 3x 90 ml drinks for our ego. My head was confusing me along with my eyes and I could have fell down anytime. I was in not in my senses.

With the 4th peg on the table Rahul said he wants pee and went into the bathroom. He stood up and as he try to manage himself to stand correctly he fall on the chair. Monty tries to help him up but he threw his hand saying; "You think I am drunk... fuck off"

I gave a smile to Krishna, I knew I too was not ok but at least I was not showing it. The things could be better if we had not taken it neat but the bet had its rule and the bottoms up was like ice on the heat vaporizing it without turning into other forms. Krishna witnessed the whole thing, smiling at our foolish act, while Monty looked wired.

We could not hear anything from Rahul's loo. So Monty went to check on him. The door was open. When Monty called out to Rahul, he turned back and pee fell on Monty's shoe.

"***Saale***"; said Monty in anger.

And the two studs started fighting there only in the bathroom.

Krishna ran towards the bathroom to end their fight but before he could enter Monty shouted aloud "You puked on me. You idiot"

Krishna saw the sight and laughed and called me. I too entered inside and cherished the site.

Two were still fighting and Monty scolding him while Rahul putting hand on his head knowing he has lost the bet. We both could laugh as much as we could with the bet currency in our hand.

Next day it was the headline for the college news about me winning a 10 rupee note from Rahul and Monty.

CHAPTER 10

———My secret friend——-

I was there at the library as hostel was not a good place to study. It had a lot of distractions there. I had many memories for Diva in my heart and it was hard for me to study there so I decided to study at library. But we usually cannot go through what we decide, while I was searching for the book I saw a lady a little older than me standing near to the book shelf searching for a particular book, she was wearing glasses. Her dress was like an angel. She was wearing white tee and blue pants. Her shirt was not big enough in length and was just kissing the upper border of her pants. While she could lift her hand to reach the book I got a good glance at her beautiful navel. Her navel ring was rather seducing. I wanted to see more of this girl. I kept looking at her and went into thought of putting my hand across her waist and touching her navel but suddenly the books from the rack moved, making space for this girl to look for the other side. She came to know that someone was enjoying her beauty. And when I saw her, she was my teacher, my angel Miss. Sehgal.

Oh God! She was really looking like a college girl. Short, sexy and in my dictionary I could not praise her with any words. However, her expression said "Idiot! You are looking at your teacher" I felt ashamed this time. I looked back into my book and it was an end of a beautiful mirage.

She went off taking the book and I don't know why I followed her to the desk.

She went into the teacher section for reading her book and I took a seat just behind her so that I could see her. She got engaged into her book while I kept looking her.

I was unaware that she was looking at me from the mirror while I was gazing her and searching for the color of her panty which was clearly visible. The girl stood up and came to me at once. I look at my watch as the library was about to close and I was relaxed about the fact that she might be going but her steps came to my table. This thing scared me.

She came next to me and with a little fishy smile she sat next to me.

"What were you looking at?" questioned Miss Sehgal with a harsh look.

"Nothing"; I reply hiding my cold sweat and shiver that I suddenly had as she sat next to me.

Her fen, her body aura was awesome and soothing.

"Well you must be looking at something or searching something... in this book, else why you are sitting here in the library for so long"; said Miss. Sehgal.

I took a deep breath as the question changed which she asked first and it was something answerable.

"Well looking for some Conceptual reading here and some of the words are tough for me, I wonder why it is the in our syllabus"; said I.

Oops some wrong line from my side and hurting for a teacher.

"Well for the student like you who looks into the things without understanding the fact"; the words were again alarming.

"I never like this subject" I went straight to my point and to hide myself and my inner consciousness of peeping at her.

"Well do you have a bike here"; she came close and whispers it while standing up.

"Ya I do"; reply I.

"Well come along with me to my flat and I'll give you a simple book, take it along and drop me home too"; said her with a little bitchy smile on her face.

I knew she had some plans. I took the bike and we drove to her place. Entering her room, she asked me if I wanted some tea and told me to be comfortable there while she put water on the pan for the tea and went into the bathroom for changing her clothes.

I kept looking her personal things and her pics. She was a real beautiful girl of her times. She had some of her pics in minis and some of the costumes were hardly wearable here at India.

"You like what you see?" she said while she came out of the washroom. I had not noticed her coming out.

I loved this sight , she was in her white transparent kurta and PJ's but I love to say her that please wear your short small skirt you are wearing in these pics so that I could see you more.

"Well I had been in UK for 8 years and these were taken there, I don't have any friends here"; said the poor girl as if she was asking me for any friendship.

"Well we can be if you don't mind" said I at once giving a hand and a shoulder to the poor girl.

"As far as it remain between two of us and bit professional too, no friendship thing at college"; said the girl.

"Sure" I reply giving a hand and a handshake took place.

We sat down while we had our tea and I got the book and I went back to my place.

I open the book and I got a clear signal. Her name was written on the page along with her number underneath.

I at once took the mobile and messaged her" Thanks"

The reply came in a minute as if she was waiting for it desperately.

"I knew you wanted this and many a times I had noticed you noticing me in the class"

The reply was positive to me.

"Study well friend" another message came clearly signaling me to concentrate more on studies and being professional. So I didn't message her thereafter.

The time came for my examinations. Clock ticking by and I could not answer anything much in the exam as I was wasting time with parties and gals. I repent a lot but all was waste. Somehow I filled the answer sheet and a bad moment ended there only with the last answer. I could proudly say that:

++"Every answer in the sheet was fictional and it has nothing to do with the course book. If something happened to match with any text book, the student was not responsible for it and was purely co incidental."++

I knew I was going to fail and someone who could help me out here was my secret friend my teacher Miss. Sehgal.

@

—And time passes very quickly until—

I wanted to make a new start here with my teacher. I wanted to be with her again and pay a visit to her house. So I made a plan. I saw her car parked outside the parking. I call up Krishna to help me out.

Krishna kept the security guard busy while I puncture the car's tyre. And then we move out of the parking waited till the college got over. Everyone was gone only I was left there alone in the parking. I even made Krishna to move out of the sight. I waited for 15 minutes till Miss. Sehgal came out finishing her college duty. I greeted her to get her attention and to show my presence.

"Manav, what you doing?" said her.

"Just "; shrugging my shoulder; I could not say anything coz of my confused expression and she did not question more.

She sat in her car and started the engine. I could see her eyes noticing me but I kept quiet and busy looking at greenery near the parking. She knew I was up to something coz my bike was missing.

She came near and to give me cold shoulder she said "Bye buddy" and started racing the car.

I wanted her to notice her punctured tyre of the car but she was going ahead anyway.

"Hey mam" I screamed aloud to stop her car.

As the car stop I went running near to it.

"Your tyre" I said huffing.

"What?"

"It's punctured"; I reply.

"Oh! I didn't notice"; said Miss. Sehgal sadly.

She came out of the car looking at the tyre.

"I think you have no choice than letting me help you out'; I said like macho, hiding my cunning intensions as they were just perfect to deceive her. I took the key and started putting the jack at car and start changing the tyre.

She took out her purse and kept herself busy by looking herself in the mobile mirror and I continue changing the tyre of the car. I could see her and praise her beauty in between and she could hardly notice me that someone is gazing at her.

"So it's perfectly fine now'; I said to her closing the door of her car door putting the puncture type inside it.

"Thanks"; said the mam.

"How are you going to go back home, it's late. You are half an hour late. I see no bike here"; said she.

"Hmm. "; I moaned slowly looking at other side.

"Let me help you out as you have helped me so much" Said Sehgal.

I gave a smile and sit along and she started to drive home back.

"My flat is on the way. Why don't you visit my room and we can have coffee? You look starved" said Sehgal.

It was a perfect thing and I nodded yes to her invitation I went along with her to her flat for the coffee and it was second time we were together alone in her house. This time my intensions were not clear and she knew it well. She change her clothes, went inside the kitchen and I started staring at her from the back. Watching her was an awesome sight and my eyes were getting use to it. She was more frank to me every time we had talked on mobile or did SMS chat. She was like a friend to me outside the college. She was a matured lady and elder than me. It was hard for me to make a start.

"Why are you always staring at me"; she said, with coffee mugs in her hand.

I really want to praise her.

"No" I said in a confused manner.

"Hey I had noticed you and your eyes speak a lot"; said Sehgal giving me a stare.

"You are a beautiful lady, you know that"; said I without thinking what might be the consequences.

"I knew that and you adore my beauty, you eyes speak it all."

Miss. Sehgal adjusted herself on the sofa next to me and turned on the TV. The equation was very simple, she had no place to sit if she wanted to watch TV she had to sit next to me. But it was honorable for me.

"Are you engaged"; I questioned her while taking a sip of my coffee to check the concentration of sugar in it.

"It is a personal question." she said as if she wants to escape from this question.

"Well I am single and I don't think any personal thing in not to be shared"; I said excitingly.

"Well I am not a teenage to love" said Sehgal lifting her collars.

"Or you are scared of doing that?"; said I to peel her little to know her more.

She seemed to be interested in me by her expression but this time I was being baseless in my talks.

"Well may be"; she said giving a hard edge and an agreement to my statement which I just flaunt.

We kept silent for some time and then I had last sip of the coffee. She took the mug and went into the kitchen. I follow her and went inside. She was near the sink washing the pan and I just went to say goodbye so that I could reach back on time to the hostel.

I saw her washing mugs while a strand of her hair touching her face. She looked very pretty and I came close to her, put my hand in her falling hair and lift the strand that was coming onto her face put it aside. She moved with the mug in the hand and looked at me.

We stared at each other for some time and her eyes glittered in dim light of the kitchen. I came close to her and my hand on her back and gave a kiss on her eyes. She closed her eyes.

I kiss her cheeks and she opened her eyes. And to my next step I came near to her lips to kiss her. She put her hand on my chest to stop me and push me away hard in anger.

"This is wrong! You are a student"; she said. I, however, was high.

It was unethical but I made one more attempt. She turned her face in a disagreement and I hugged her tight.

"Sorry Manav you are a really very nice friend and let's not end it up with something like this"; she whispered in my ears.

I stopped my lusty overtures and said "Friends forever"

"Yes if we keep a distance..."

I moved back to my room and latched it. Lighted my cigarette, took a deep puff, and looked at the wall thinking what I was about to do... was it right, I was about to commit a sin.

Beeps

I looked at the screen. It was my teacher's message, I open.

"Thanks Manav, my best friend you can ask me for help anytime... It's hard to find a true friend ship, hope we don't lose it for sake for any other relationship like this which has no name and is wrong..."

It was the first time I understood my teacher and what she wanted me to understand.

I message her back

"You stopped me and I am thankful... else I would have committed a sin"

And yes it was a sin, going out with a teacher.

Many of us may have their first crush be their teacher only but it is a weird situation, still fine up to a level. But if you keep on going through such feelings and turn them into real relationships, definitely you will land up into a big problem in the end.

"You will get your girl definitely, just wait for the right time" message beeped again.

"Wish… to' I reply her with a bye message altogether and a bad phase ended before it could get worse.

CHAPTER 11

THE SETTLEMENT

——Gauri my senior——

"So what will you like to have?" asks Gauri while looking at the menu card.

"Nothing I am not much into eating here"; reply I.

"I just came here to spend a little time with you"; I continued giving her more importance than food.

Gauri felt shy because of my words which could be easily noticeable by her face which looked so beautiful.

"So you punctured Miss. Sehgal's car?" said Gauri to me.

"You are a naughty guy"; she continues.

"What else are you up to?"

"Nothing much "; I said while laughing.

"Who told you?"

"Krishna"; reply Gauri.

"But it was a secret"

"And you went to her flat'; said Gauri before I could defend myself.

'For the coffee..."

"I know all and let's not talk about it"; said Gauri being serious this time and a lil' upset.

I too try to skip this conversation.

"It's between three of us and the teacher who don't know two of us know it. So let's keep your secret a secret only'; said Gauri to support me.

I did not say anything. I kept shut and had my food.

"When my exams will be over I will be going to US and it will hard to be in contact for at least for 2-3 months"; said Gauri.

"Ok" this I could only say at this time as I was feeling like a culprit.

"Where is Krishna?" I questioned Gauri and to change this topic.

"Gone for some interview"

"Ok" I said again.

And then we had our food without saying anything else. While we were going to our rooms back to our hostel we had a walk and it was so romantic. And I remember few months back when I came to the college how I messed up with this girl...

@1st Interaction with Gauri few months back

"Hey look at the lovely gal in the ATM"; I said to Binnie. Whatever I was doing to my life; what I did with Meha for Diva and what I was doing with other relations. Now I was like another boy around trying on every girl who so ever comes after a good startup classes from Karan. For us every girl is beautiful someone has good face, good height, good attitude or nature and may have good sizes.

I could not resist myself talking to the girl. She looked pretty. And I had only two things as qualifications first was gals and second was beautiful cute gals and she fulfills both the criteria.

"Well with the plaster on"; I continues pointing towards the ATM.

"C'mon Manav you can't even get near her"; said Binnie challenging me, as the girl was too good for me and I knew it but I was confident about my charm over the girls. You may consider it over confidence but I never look back when I decide.

"You think so?" I ask Binnie with a big O on my face and a question mark.

"Yeah I am pretty sure you cannot"; said Binnie adding oil to the fire.

++ Some one wisely said: For Boys challenges not accepted it's a ***karo or maro*** situation for them.++

"Laggi 500 ki"; I said to Binnie putting it as a bet.

This was the time I was over confidence to my charm.

"Well! look at me when you see me there, talking to the girl and tell me when I call her cute gal"; said I to Binnie with collars up.

To the start I took out my ATM card from my pocket and went inside the ATM booth. It was written to be in a queue and one at a time but still I swap my card and went inside with a smile at my face.

"Hi"; I said to the girl.

It was silly as I look back from here.

"Hi' I said again increasing the pitch of my voice as I could not get a reply for my first one, looking at the girl with the plaster on struggling with the ATM machine. She looked at me at this situation one how one can ask for an intro.

"HI"; said girl without looking at me keeping herself busy with the machine.

"Well, this is a Colles fracture?" I ask her while describing the type.

"As the orthopedics says"; reply the girl with a grin.

"Okay good"; I reply back excited at least the talks are on.

"What????" the girl looked back this time to see my face.

"No I mean the work done on it is good" I tried escaping the embarrassment with a sudden reply from my side.

"No I mean the written over it is good" pointing towards the signatures and quotation written over the plaster, some girlish work done to make it lil interesting.

"I wonder how can girls be so silly as to do make up of a plaster to match it with her clothes or so" I said to myself.

"These… my friends did" said girl with a smile.

"As a good luck" she continues.

"Okay"

"So you reside at Hostel no 5"; I try different question this time.

"No"

"6" I asks.

"No"

"7"; I asks again.

"What do you want mister" said the girl as I was being more ***chaip*** to the girl.

"Your address"; I said with a smile.

"I mean if I say Lemme help you with the ATM machine. You will probably call me for a coffee"; I continue.

"For a coffee?" she could not control her smile this time.

"Then I will let you go to your hostel too like a gentleman" I continue with my silly conversation.

"So I am asking?" said I justifying myself and my question.

Pause

"Oh I didn't introduce myself how can we go for a coffee"; I said like a despo.

"Lemme Introduce myself to you then it will be bit easier for us";

I try being gentle now.

"Myself Hardik"; I said in advance with a wrong name and made her a bit uncomfortable. I always learned from Binnie and Karan if you are flirting with a girl; never give your real name to her.

Nothing was working out and I was just looking like an Idiot as I didn't notice myself.

Pause and girl thought for a while.

"What you said you name Hard dick" girl being more cheesy and in a no way compromising mood.

"No I said Hardik"; I try again.

"Ohkay! Whatever"; said girl.

"You can call me Rahul… All my friends call me this; Sanorita"; I try Shharukh's voice DDLJ this time to lighten her mood.

"I try to escape what happen now" as I was being more of a headache to the girl.

"What??"

"Rahul"; I utter again.

"Owl…"; reply girl making fun of me again.

I knew the girl was playing with words but at least she was smiling and she look <OMG> dam beautiful.

"Look I got a smile on your face"; said I to the girl.

"I always had one"; she reply back.

As a reply of my flirting, I knew she was angry on me for what I said so much to her in a few minutes.

"Well I can help myself"; said girl as the money came from the machine.

Giving a smile; She uttered; "Bye Manav. I know you, am Krishna's friend and for the rest of information you asking for, ask him."

"I am your senior by the way"; said girl while opening the ATM's door.

"Sorry mam" I said aloud.

She turns back and gave a smile to me and nodding a No with her head. I put my hands on my hair thinking shit what I had done try being stud.

My end was near as we all know if someone messes with seniors, he is definitely gonna land up with a huge problem and that's what I did now. I ran towards other side try opening my contacts in the mobile.

I dial Krishna's number.

Rings

"What?"; said Krishna getting disturbed; at these hours as he was in the library studying.

"I mean your friend who got a plaster on, what's her name?" I ask.

Krishna tries memorizing a bit.

"Oh her, her name is Gauri"; reply Krishna.

"Okie"

"I think I messed up with her… a bit"; said I.

"Again… with how many people are you gonna play pranks and I will not be always there for your rescue"; say Krishna.

"C'mon help me this time. I will not do it again"

"Every time the same statement"; reply Krishna to my fake promises.

"Ok don't worry she's a good friend I will take care of the rest"; says Krishna.

"Now you please don't mess up with someone again bro"; continue him.

"Okie Bro"

And the call ends…

Binnie at other corner near around hearing the conversation and with a smile on his face

"As Binnie says" says Binnie aloud dramatically looking at the sky:
"Har scene aur Har film ka hero tu thode ho sakta hai…"

Laughed Binnie as he knew everything, she was our senior and it was a prank.

"500 bucks fast"; said Binnie to me.

I try putting my hand in my back pocket to search for my purse. Before I could get it…

"We'll keep the change"; said Binnie to me laughingly.

I knew my first impression on the girl was bad but I have to accept it. And I was pretty assured that I would never ever gonna get near to this girl in the nearby future.

Beep with a message I was back into reality in front of her hostel smiling

A message came and I look into my mobile it was my secret friend.

"Hey how was your exam" message came from other side.

It was my Miss. Sehgal's message.

"Nothing good is happening here"; I type back.

This was something happening from the past few weeks and we had conversation over anything to everything and we even had talk about sex and anything including my seducing fantasies for her and Miss Sehgal was actually enjoying it now.

This was my last exam and I was excited to go home for a while.

"I am going home at the end of this week" I message to my teacher.

"Then you should come once to my room to meet me" reply came from other side.

I wanted to meet this lady for a while as she was also moving to UK for next PHD degree and I was the one who was going to miss her more than my college.

"When are you coming?" asks my teacher.

"Tomorrow will be fine with me"; I reply and we end the call by passing good notes to each other.

@

—Next day—

Early morning as I knew she will not be going to the college, I went to her room to meet her. I knock the door. Her bai opens the door and made me sit to the room kept as the drawing room of her flat. I ask her bai for her.

"Memsaab is bathing" said bai and "I am going. I have finished work."

"And tell memsaab doodh is there in the kitchen" she continued and left the place.

Now I was left alone at her flat. I went to her room where we usually sat and I start looking at her personal stuff. Her clothes were lying there on the bed and I could hear the noise of the shower coming out of the bathroom and I could imagine her nude bathing.

While I was staring at her clothes, suddenly the door opens and to my surprise she came outside with the towel. I could see her naked legs as the towel only touched the upper knee of her body and I could feel the aroma of her soap. And it was the most pleasant sight of my life. She was semi nude in front of me and I could not react. I started shivering from inside. Her body was like a fish and so tender to touch. I felt like my lever was hard for her and everything between me and her vanished with the thought as I came close to her. She could find herself in trouble in front of me.

"Bai has gone"; I said while gazing at her body and her little fine cups and make her feel comfortable.

I intentionally say it so that she should know that we are alone at her flat and it is the right time that we should now forget the baseline and should cross it.

I made a hard move and come close to her. She tries to hide herself and dig her beautiful body into that little towel. I put my hand around her tender waist and she could not say anything. She kept quit and gave me way to enter. I push her wet body close to me, so close that even not the air could cross between us. Her cups touch hard onto my chest and my tool touches her.

I kiss her on her beautiful neck and she moaned "Manav stop it…."

But Manav now was hard to be stopped here. I could feel her warm breath which was gaining more and more momentum as I kiss her on either side of her neck and to a smart move I give her a little bite on her ears. She moans to it. I push her to the bed which gave a blow to her towel too. She crosses her legs as the wrap of the towel got loosen up due to the fall. I came over her. My hand held her hand and the body gluing each other I looked into her eyes and gave her a kiss on her lips and as I start sucking her lips and she also responded well to me. We kiss each other for several minutes and then I came onto her privates and a perfect first timer oral happened between us two with the fall of her love nectar.

"Are we doing right..."; said she with her voice showing her urge and repentance.

I held her hand while lying on her side. I kiss her and gave her an assurance that the thing will remain buried between us two.

Looking to the roof and Miss. Sehgal lying side to me I said:

I can still feel your kisses
setting fire to my soul
ordeal diminishing my body
and leaving me to a thirst
wanting you, needing you
a feeling where a breath is theft
Loving each other
until there is no choice left
your skin on mine
no choice
feeding off the heat
no choice
crashing into each other
no choice

until we couldn't tell
where you ends and I began
and so we collapsed together,

freezing this moment
laughing and talking
and being silly...

forgetting everything
with this time being running out...

And then she didn't say again whether we are doing anything bad and kept enjoying the beautiful moment. We both hugged each other for hours and enjoyed each other's company.

CHAPTER 12

THE REVENGE

It was hard time for Rahul and Monty. I knew they were into revenge to charge me against that 10 rupee note and provoked me a lot to sit together with the bet again for it. But I was also too cunning to sit along with them for that till the day when I could not say no to them for exchange of drinks again.

——Fuckin' Life @ Hostel 5———

It was a holiday and we had nothing to do. At noon a party was decided. It started with two of us- Krishna and Me from one side; Monty and Rahul at other. But this time Monty was also competing from one end. It was a simple daru party till again our egos clashed. It was a self portrait plot for me from the two bastards at the other side. They somehow court me into their plot and we had bet for the hard dirty drinking in their format. It was a format of drinking the mixing pattern where a mixed drink was unethically made. Different kind of alcohol – Rum, Vodka, and Wine along with coffee powder, butter and soda were used to make the drinks. I knew this thing could kill us as it was unbearable to the body and its physiology. But the party started and drinks were served and no one had the time to back off. As a first starter we have 2x 60-60ml pegs and we gulped it without thinking.

In a minute we started to confuse our selves. The thing was so concentrated that I with difficulty try to manage myself and the third drink got served on the table. It was 30ml peg so I did a bottoms up again like everyone in the company. I knew this was the last thing I could manage. I stood up quitting the bet there only but I knew the things had gone out of control. I fell down the floor un-conscious.

Everything seemed a blur to my vision. I felt as if my heart beat was slowing down. I could feel the coldness and numbness to my hands and foot. I knew it is the end. I could see a white light in front of my eyes. My heart beat was getting slower still. I could hear people around me calling my name but I was frozen helplessly like my body was paralyzed. I could not tell them what I was feeling. I felt like I was dying. I could see a bright, white light and seemed to be coming closer and as it engulfed me I felt as if I was travelling down a well with white walls. I can remember thinking when will I reach the end of this journey and then my vision slowly faded until I could remember nothing.

When I opened my eyes, I found myself on the floor, of a white room. I stood up and looked at the other side of the room. I was standing in front of Gauri. She stood at other end looking at me where as I stood in the center of the room. Everything was so pleasant and there was a pin drop silence. I touched my face to see as if I am alive. Then I looked at Gauri. We looked into each other's eyes. Gauri was all white. Her face seemed as if had been painted white and she was wearing a white beautiful dress. She looked like a witch. I got scared as I saw a lot of mascara applied to her eyes. Her mascara was tracked down her cheeks as if she had cried a lot. It was all ruined with tears.

"Why do you drink so much?"

"Are you punishing yourself?"

"And for whom?" questioned Gauri.

I could not answer and just kept looking at her eyes. Her eyes were boring a hole through me. I felt like I had no answers to her questions. I inhaled deeply. I could not hear anything else. The only thing I could notice were her long black painted nails. I wished to skip this site but I could not. My feet did not move. I look at the other side to ignore her and ignore her questions. Then another familiar voice came from another side. When I looked behind I saw Diva surprisingly standing there trying to say something to me but I could not hear. So I tried to concentrate more on her lips and tried to read them. I could now hear her voice. I could hear my name uttered with pain.

"Yes"; reply I scared.

She was wearing a red dress looking as beautiful as always like a newlywed bride.

"I don't know what you are doing to yourself but our best days are far behind us and you are just chasing a time which you cannot hold." Diva said to me in pain. Her face was also white and her eyes also had a lot of kajal put into them. I could not describe the culture these ladies were following using a lot of mascara and kajal on their eyes but it was scary.

Then I saw someone standing behind her but her face was not clear. I tried to concentrate on her.

She was Meha…

Her blurred face became clear as I concentrated more on her. The thought of the Diva vanished in a second. I was standing in front of the very sour truth of my life. Meha was the one I had betrayed. I was a culprit. She was the one I could never face. I knew I used her all my life and she never complained to me about it.

Meha requested me; "Why don't you love me back?"

"Because I love her…"; I point towards Diva where she was standing waiting for a reply from my side.

"Who?"

"She, can't you see her?"

But as I tried to point at Diva to show her the girl; no one was there. Diva was gone. I cried out aloud. I felt like someone was pinching me from inside and putting something in my mouth.

Suddenly I open my eyes. I was lying on a bed with so many people surrounding me. I was in a critical situation. I was in the hospital's emergency with doctors treating me for alcohol poisoning.

What I just saw was just a dream but also the truth of my life. I was still having difficulty in breathing.

"Do the ***gastric levarge*** immediately"; "need to empty his stomach" shouted someone.

"Let him vomit"; said Doctor from other side as I turned to vomit out the toxicant.

"This will help"

As I continuously vomited for sometime till I felt dehydrated but I felt a little relief as well.

"Give him saline I.V"

I could hear only this and I passed out again. I could hear the beeping sound and then all of a sudden nothing was audible and I fell asleep.

I don't remember further what happened to me and next morning. I woke up in the ICU with Krishna looking at me, waiting for me to come into my senses.

"How did I come here?" I asked as I tried to move and adjusted myself a little.

"You want me to start with all what happened at yesterday's party"; reply Krishna.

"I picked you up from the floor and I admitted you to the emergency"

"Look what you have done to yourself"

"I kept telling you not to do that stuff and you drunk so much that you got sick" Krishna yelled at me.

"I will never do it again"; said I as I hugged Krishna like my elder brother.

You know Krishna said "Our teacher, who is going back to U.K called you. I did not tell her your condition".

"Thank you but I know she is going" I replied.

"You knew that earlier"; said Krishna.

And I gave a witty smile along with a fuckin' sign.

"You are a dog"; said Krishna with a silly expression on his face.

I knew I was losing a friend and I was ship wrecked again. And a bad episode ends...

The Confession

To all the girls I met, I adore you the most
Where ever I go there you are
This memory of yours is just a host...
I love you each day, and adore you the most...

People may say why you are punishing yourself
I would rather say, this is how I am vanishing myself...
To give you a stay, this is what I pray
Something I would say
When I came to know you... you left

To all the girls I slept, I adore you a lot
Something I could not met, I love you the most
And most is the something; I could not get ...

Should I now feel guilty of something.. Should I bet
I am just on bank of the river, where you never met
I draw myself into sea of tear,
And gradually I lose you
I realize I really miss you...
But it's now been a year

"Should I beg when I want you back..."

With all my tears,

Mani

CHAPTER 13
WHY IT HAPPENS

End of the degree

Mobile rings

It was my teacher and her last call as she was leaving.

"Meet me for the last time"; said Miss Sehgal orderly.

As "IT" has happened between us and I knew what we owed each other. That noon I went to her flat.

As I she opens the door I could see the mood being created in the room. Sehgal was looking as seductive as she could. I had never seen her look so sexy. Her room freshener was my favorite jasmine. The room was all clear as everything was packed. Candles were lit and were placed near the bed, windows and on the table. A perfect ambience as we say. I looked at her as she opened the door she was wearing white knickers with a transparent tee.

As I enter the house Sehgal closed the door and we could not resist hugging like we were starved of each other.

"Hardcore, I want it this way" said Sehgal with lust in her eyes hugging me tight.

I look at her. I could not understand her words.

"I know what you want and searching in me from past few days and I am ready to give what you want"; Sehgal said looking into my eyes.

"I want you to love me with your lust which is visible in your eyes and I want to see how much you can"; she continues.

She knew this was the last time and she wanted it to be memorable. I came close. She was different from every girl I had been. I knew she was not my love. I just had lust for her. Something still pious and secretively I was approaching her knowing we are doing it just as we were fulfilling each other's need in every way.

As I slid my hand from behind I was all prepared for the move but she was a little more practical than I could imagine. Her sex knowledge was more than I had and so I was just a student in front of her.

"Come close and I will take you to heaven", she said like she possessed me and I could sense her passion.

"How?" I asked enquiringly and desperate to know.

"Shut up! You are not supposed to ask me" as she threw me hard on the bed.

I kept mum. I, being desperate, could not control myself. Sex was not new to me but the way she was going about it, was different and I didn't know how not to behave like a lil' virgin in front of her. But thanks to my first interaction with an experienced lady who was introducing me to this world. I followed her command.

As she unbuttoned my shirt I just lay there with my arms open looking her into her eyes as she moved her lips over my chest and kissed me everywhere. I could see the lust in her eyes. I was helpless in front of her beauty. Her dominance challenged my manhood I got hold of her hair hard and made her come on top of me fully. As her lips hit mine I kissed her hard to fulfill my thirst for her. She also kissed me on my lips and they were perfect to suck. I held her hard over me and she just enjoyed me. I tried unbuttoning her knickers.

"Wait a minute" as she ran to the kitchen with her unbuttoned knickers and half worn tee and her hair loose, touching her body. It was a passionate sight.

I raised my head to see what she was up to now.

She came running with chocolate ice cream in her hand and threw it on my chest.

"I wanna lick it all" she says as she put that cold chocolate ice cream over me.

With some cream on her hand she put it in my mouth and I sucked it hard and then she sucked the same finger. I then sucked her lips as I wanted to taste her part of the chocolate which was sweetest thing I could ever get.

And then she licked the rest of the chocolate ice cream spilt over me and teased me till I beg for more.

She unbuttoned my pants as I opened her shirt altogether with her bra and threw her nude body over mine. The chocolate cream was now on us both and we started licking each other's ice cream and then we crashed on each other.

Lying beside her naked body with her in my arms and looking at the ceiling and thinking what we were doing a minute ago.

"You want a cigarette?" said Sehgal to me as she lighted one for herself.

"I'll have from this one" I replied back pointing the cigarette in her hand.

After two puffs Sehgal headed me her lighted cigarette as she searched for the ashtray.

++ As we know: Whatever the situation is, Girls are always disciplined.++

I took a puff and as Sehgal slid herself over me to reach the ashtray kept on my side table I kissed her body in response to which, Sehgal kissed my lips.

"Thanks for this time"; said Sehgal handing me the ashtray.

"You should not be, I learnt a lot from you"; I replied back.

"You are very particular about this ash" I said pouring the ash into the tray.

"I am particular about you too"; said Sehgal caressing me.

"When am I gonna have a poem again from you like our first day."

"Soon"; I said taking a puff.

"One thing" said Sehgal to me as she clicked a pic of me with her mobile, sliding her head close to me to be in the frame.

"For the memories we share"; she utter.

"You know what…"

"Mani, I had changed your result myself, your marks were very low not even passing but I did it on my own risk, I helped you all the way to the borderline so please don't expect good marks"; said Miss. Sehgal to me seriously this time.

"Ok, mam"; I replied obediently.

She was leaving so it was necessary that I should show some respect for her, the one who made my life.

"And whatever happened between us, it is very memorable for me so please let us end it all, as there's no future so we will maintain a professional relationship forever"; she said in a way which was quite persuasive.

I held her hand in my hand as always and she put her head over my chest.

"We are ending this"; said Sehgal, a little disheartened.

"For good" I said.

"Yeah" and she kissed me again and left me on the bed alone, and went to the bathroom.

She was nude and my eyes followed her as she moved around to change. As she reached near the door of the bathroom to enter she looked back and caught me red-handed, gazing at her nude body.

"This is what Mani… that makes me mad"

"You had already got me. Then why are you gazing"; she continues.

"You are beautiful"; I replied back.

"Way older than you"; she smiled.

"But mine"; said I romantically.

"Love you" and this was the first time I heard such a thing from Sehgal.

And she entered the bathroom and I thought "Does she love me or it was just lust?"

Whatever it was, it ended and Sehgal wanted it to end and so did I.

"Ok mam, it will remain in my heart forever and the sweet memories will be there and will never come out" I said shouting from outside to her reply for Love.

"Your result will be out this week so have fun, am leaving tonight at 3'o clock"; she says and we exchange our email address afterwards.

"Will remain in contact forever"; said she while I packed my stuff to leave her place.

I was pretty relaxed about the whole thing as if a nightmare had ended as the things going on between us were ethically wrong and if such a thing comes out it would end my career and my life.

—The result—

Finally came the day, the most awaited day of my life... the day for result as per my efforts in the bed with my teacher it was quite known I will pass although many of my ***masti*** friends they could not make it to the mark and they still wondered how I was passed when I was with them all day and night having fun. The first person I remembered here was Miss. Sehgal who was missing from my life. She had gone to UK by the night flight the day we had our last conversation.

Result was out and I passed; now it was my senior's convocation time and I was invited by Gauri. Something fishy was still there on Gauri's side. She had known about my sexual encounters with Miss. Sehgal; as I respected and loved this girl I didn't hesitate in telling her everything which happened by mistake between us.

Gauri still knew that in our first interaction at ATM, I was trying to hit on her. It was quite noticeable by my flirty attitude towards her that I wanted to propose to her. But her decision to be my girlfriend was not clear. I wanted this thing to be crystal clear as I was in love with her and yes it was true and there was nothing like I had for other girls who enters my life and made it upside and down.

I never wanted to propose to her as I was afraid of the fact that if she didn't like hearing that I had a crush on her, it would end my friendship with her. But her charming talks would confuse me sometimes, she started talking in such a caring way that it made me feels that there's something between us.

Sometimes her jealousy at me talking to other girls would make me think point that I should now make a start with her.

In the last days I could not do anything other than helping her pack her bags and taking her out for dinner for the last time and she went home the next morning. And to my self-disgust when it was time to make memories with her I made myself busy with other work and ignored her. She didn't talk much after that.

We were meeting after such a long time at the convocation and it was the best time to tell her how I felt as the distance between us was taking toll on our friendship. I decided that I should tell her as this was my only chance with this girl.

++Some wise words: If you love someone admit it; there may be a chance to lose but if you don't confess you have no chance else than losing.++

And to my good luck for the very first time I was called upon by Gauri at the time of her convocation or maybe she was giving me a last chance to express myself and my feelings for her.

++ Someone has said: Girls know the feeling but it is still needs to be elaborated.++

Gauri called me intentionally to make me propose to her. She called me for some petty work which she could have done herself. It was clear that once again she was giving me a chance to express myself.

Finally the convocation day came....

The day came when everyone gathered for the convocation in the University hall. It was noon and the day was hotter than usual making me tense too. I took a seat next to Gauri. She was with her friend. As I was taking my place her hand touched mine and we both looked at each other, confused. I didn't knew where and when to start. I only knew she has given me a chance and I had to propose to her there in the hall.

A teacher on the Dice spoke memorized lines to start the function by calling the names of the students and one by one inviting them to the stage. Gauri waited for her name to be called upon. Not even the ace was helping me out this time. Gauri giving me signals to speak up something.

I said "Where to start from but I think..." trying to start the conversation.

Gauri looked at me and tried to listen what I wanted to say, nodding her head in agreement that she's interested in what I am saying.

"Ever since from the first day, when I saw you, I had this thing in my mind one day this beautiful gal will be my friend." said I confidently.

"I am"; said Gauri, along with me and as I played with my words and looked for a line that would make her understand that I am proposing to her although skipping the three words which were hard for me to speak for my favorite senior.

"Well you are confusing me"; I lost eye contact and looked down at the floor.

"C'mon you know what, even a mother doesn't feed her child if the child doesn't cries for it and if you want an answer you need to ask me for that"; said Gauri, initiating the start again.

"Yeah" I look at her eyes again.

"So the thing is, I know this might be wrong; my cards are open in front of you and you may think what kind of person I am"; I said all together.

"I feel very easy in front of you, listen to me, you care for me and this is something that makes you adorable"; I said, making a statement.

"And I was thinking if the moments spent with you are so memorable, then why don't we make them more memorable by spending more time together"

"A life time"; I continue.

"We are together; we will be in contact Mani" replied Gauri back to me.

"I mean not in the way like we are"; said I.

"Then?" Gauri questioned.

"Like a Gf and Bf… I mean if there is any possibility"; I asked her and waited for the reply, I knew I looked kiddish at time asking such a question.

And I stare at her lips searching for an answer. Gauri stood up. I look at her to see what she is up to.

"What?"; I asks again.

Gauri didn't say anything.

"My name was just announced and I am going on the stage"; said Gauri as she stood from her chair.

"And I will give you my answer soon when I come back"; said Gauri smiling.

"I think you can wait that much if you say lifetime…"; said Gauri.

"Yes I can wait for a life time, you take your time I am here only looking at you and waiting for you to come back with the same smile and an answer"; said I replying back to her words.

The signal was green I knew it with her smile.

"That smile on your face signals that you need me; I am blessed with love again. Oh! God forgive me for what I did to others" I said to myself.

I knew she was the kind of girl who will catch me where ever I fall. She wasn't just my senior. It was just she was the perfect girl around.

As Gauri starts moving towards the stage, I kept watching her. I was lost in the time. Waiting to hold her and never let go. Time seemed to be frozen. I felt my mobile was vibrating in my pocket.

Rings

I look at the screen of my mobile. It shook my head. I got goose bumps. I could not react on looking at the name on the screen.

Diva was calling me. Her name was beeping on my screen. I picked up her call with my fingers crossed.

"Hello"; said Diva from other side of the line in a numb way.

"Hello" reply I.

"Can I talk to you for a while Mani"; said Diva in an apologizing way.

I was all surprised and stunned. I could not react to anything. I was in no contact with her for the past few months. She was all busy with Kabir. I had given her my last decision to leave her with my last letter then why was she calling me and I wonder from where she got my number. I gifted my soul to her and she sold it for a relationship and a guy who never cared for her.

I could hear crying sound from the other end. Diva was crying and she tried hard hiding it but hiding her tears from inside was tough. I could feel the pain she had in her heart this time.

"What happened Diva?" I ask worried.

I knew I was no one for her now but the old habit of caring for her was still there. I managed to ask her why she was crying when I knew I had no right to ask her anything.

"I just want to say, as you always said that where ever you go, whatever you do , you will never forget me and do I still have a chance to be back?" said Diva confessing her crime.

Her crime was unforgettable. She was culprit of all those sleepless night. If I had a chance to go back I could have but I just had now proposed to Gauri and I was in a cherry mood waiting for Gauri's reply. I did not want such a thing to happen right now to me.

"I can't understand you"; said I ending my conversation with Diva.

"Can you come outside the hall"; Diva asked me for a favor.

"Where are you?" I enquired in a fuzzy manner.

The girl had traveled all the way from her place to my college just to talk with me. To confess and share the words of love with me and it was hard to turn a blind eye. I knew it was hard to believe that she loved me so much that she came here for me but I still could not believe myself and my luck that she was standing outside.

"What do you mean"; I enquire again.

To confirm her words I asked her once more.

"Yes outside the hall I wanna talk"; said Diva ordered as she used to.

I put down the line, look at the stage. Gauri was still waiting for her number to receive her degree and a photograph with vice chancellor. I could not walk even a single step but somehow I managed to go out while Gauri from the stage kept watching me.

She expected me to be there standing in front row when she received her degree. It was a special moment for her and she wanted me to be there standing but I was leaving and turning her good time into a bad one like always.

I came out of the hall searching for Diva. Diva was standing under the sun looking as beautiful as always and my heart skipped a beat. I felt like I was meeting her for the first time. I came close to her. Before I could say anything or enquire, Diva…

"This isn't hard if we start"; Diva said with a tear rolling down her cheek.

"As I looked deeper into my heart and scratch myself a bit. I find myself trying to get something which was never mine and trying to hurt what I had in my life"; words came so easily from Diva. But true…

"You know when I started questioning myself. It didn't take long for me to break down coz I was cheating on you and myself too"; cried out Diva this time. She was all in tears.

Her tears were shining on her cheeks under the sun like a pearl. I wanted her to cry for me like I had cried for her. It relieved me at least.

"I could never find my happiness in Kabir"; said Diva.

"Now what is that supposed to mean"; said I.

"I never think about it, but I didn't come clean like you. I just told you the story behind the story. You left me... May be its better for you, but I am fading each day as I am away from you…" Diva confessed her pain to me.

"I want you back" Continue Diva.

"You think it's funny"; said I.

"No! But I am now trying to make the best of a bad situation I created"

"I am just trying"

"I think you are pissed off and trying to get something out of nothing." I replied to her to tell her that the time is gone when I needed her the most.

"I know I am left empty handed" said Diva.

As I was talking to her, behind her, I saw Gauri standing outside the hall looking at me, as she came closer from other end searching for me.

"Are you guys going out?" said Gauri.

Gauri, with a smile on her face...

It was a fake one I could see but it hurt very much thinking Gauri must be hurt.

I would like to introduce you to..." said I, as I search for an appropriate word.

Before I could say anything more, Gauri continuing my sentence "best friend"

"You must be Diva right?" said Gauri looking at her.

"Ya"; Diva looked at her strangely.

"You know what, there was never a day when Mani hasn't talk about you, I wished to see you"; said Gauri to Diva.

"To see someone who could be so much loved"; said Gauri while looking into my eyes.

I broke the eye contact and looked down. It was very painful looking back into her eyes.

"No one deserves you better than Mani"; said Gauri with a smile, Diva too smiled back.

Gauri was helping Diva in her reconciliation with me.

"Why don't you shake hands? And I guess you guys need some space"; said Gauri while moving out.

"I think I must go"; uttered Gauri while moving away from me and then she never looked back.

I kept watching her but she didn't turn back. I wanted to call Gauri back but I could not as my tongue got paralyzed. I move other way while Diva follow me and Gauri went her own way.

Mobile beeps

It was Gauri's SMS. I open the message.

It was: "I know you love her, so don't let her go, you have done a lot for her"

Reading the message, I held Diva's hand, looked into her eyes and hugged her as Gauri words make me realize how much I love her. I was running away from myself when I was running away from Diva.

As I hugged her, the thought of Gauri came in to my mind and I push her away from me. Diva looked into my eyes searching for the reason.

"I thought I was charming"; said Diva.

"Yeah baby you are still charming and close to my heart"; I rely back.

"But I have to had a talk to Gauri"; I continued.

Diva was confused.

I went inside her hostel, I ran towards Gauri's room. The room where her stuff was made was locked. She was gone and this thought was killing me that I could not meet her, I ran towards the parking. I could see her car starting to move. I was far away from her but still I tried to run behind it thinking I might reach her.

I could not reach what I was running for, I knew it. I cried aloud Gauri's name. The car didn't stop and she was gone away. I could see her eyes noticing me from the view mirror of the car as she looked back at me from there. Our eyes met. I could not run anymore I was breathless. I stopped but the car kept moving. I lift my hand to wave at the car and she gave me the signal back by waving her hand out of the car.

Diva came close to me.

"What?" questioned Diva, still confused.

"That's true Love"; said I huffing.

"Love, true in nature.... Sacrifice as its cost... the one we love need not be with us… love should be there always…"

"Love is when you let go and even in your absence, your presence is felt".

Diva was unable to say anything and kept listening to what I was saying.

I imagine how many hearts I had hurt to get Diva in my life.

I looked at Diva. She was looking down and I was thinking ***"Was she worth it"***

Diva was with me anyway and always, but at what cost...

"As long as you hate me
I will try my best to make you
fall in LOVE with me again
Make you cry for me once
To see the tears in your eyes
A cry from your side
Saying' you owe me"

"As long as I love you
I will let you hurt me
As much as you will hurt me
I will be with you

As long as you are gone

I will miss you like anything

As long as I miss you

I will not forget you.

As long as I remember you

I will love you... And it will happen always"

Now as I look up at sky: "I see clouds; they are bluer than they always look. Sun is hotter and burning. A wind of joy has blown with tears for a loss with an unexpected end. Losing a friend, a lover for someone I loved for years; as I wanted Diva to be a part of my life but am I doing the right thing here…Is this justice to someone who took so much care of you. Someone who held you when they knew you are imperfect, why this sky is clearer now, why? "

A relation with so many sacrifices…

CHAPTER 14

BEHIND THE SCENE

Kahani Abhi Baaki Hai Mere Dost

Me and Payal on the Date *Don't tell me itna to chalta hai…*

Someone who never changed was me and my POLY-GIRL-FREND-IA syndrome. With so much happening in my life I was still in the search mode. As they always say Men are always men. It took few efforts to be here:

@

—Canteen—-

"What to order?" I ask Payal holding her hand being romantic.

"Anything Sameer sir. Whatever you wish"; replied Payal; looking into my eyes.

Confused?? Aw! My endless efforts to my new junior help me to get a date with her. And well my name had not changed, just for fun now girls calls me Sameer. Well I confess I use this name for flirting. It can be anything whichever comes first, who cares.

One thing was for sure at least my subject notes were helping me some where as they never helped me in examinations.

"Well Coffee for two"; I ordered aloud to the canteen boy.

"So where were we?" asks Payal.

"Holding hands and looking into each other's eyes" I said flirting with the girl.

The girl felt shy and I kept looking at her. I was now not new to this love game. Innocence was long gone. It was time to hit on every girl on the way.

Suddenly I felt a hand on my shoulder. I turn back.

"So Jay Happy B'day Bro"; it was sudden that Rohit was wishing me.

"Hey Rohit nice joke"; I replied back.

"You know my name, it's Sameer. If you wanna get introduced to the girl you can"; I said smiling.

"Happy B'day Jay"; Monty wishes me from other side.

Payal kept looking at me confused as I had just earned her trust.

"Actually they are playing a prank on me" I tried to explain to Payal.

"Happy B'day Bro"; said Binnie. And it was something which made me angry.

"***Saale tu bhi***..." I said to Binnie.

Binnie being my friend was playing along with other people I never cared of and they were actually destroying my reputation in front of Payal, which I could not bear.

As Binnie moved aside I could see Kartika with a hockey in his hand and full of anger looking at me.

I had no choice.

"Move Payal you can go now. This silly date is over, go"; said Monty being rude to her.

"And his name is Manav- the stud"; said Kartika to the girl as she reaches near the door.

Payal left the place and didn't even care to look back as she came to know I was fooling her.

I looked at Kartika; I knew he was hurt by my prank.

"You were right Love is very beautiful"; I tried to explain and flipped the topic.

"***Maar yahan pe khayega ya store room main***"; Kartika said only this with the hockey in his hand.

"***Store room main***" and I and started moving.....

Note from the Author:

How the book begin:

I was writing on some very serious stuff which may come out in the future to read, I was asked by my fans when are they going to get hands on another love story. I could not answer it as I could not think about any plot. Then I started with few lines about the time spent with my girl friend which were turned into chapters where Diva is shown along with Manav and their love for each other. And one day with a dream where I got enlightened with blue print of my story... I kept writing everything and saving it to my desktop which took the shape of a book with little efforts and polishing it further.

Most of the incidents in the book are not true but the healthy feeling which I went through my love life helped me to express my feelings and love, which is penned down in the book.

I again want to thank my lil' sweet gf for the breakup that made me a man otherwise I would have been the same. For me my world always revolved around her and I could not think anything else but now I have a life to live...

Thanks to all who discouraged me with their words, all the way strengthening me and my thoughts to go with my work further...

First reader: Let us start with the plot what I find is the basic thing that attaches the readers to the text. The soul of the book Love, hard to define just the most pious thing to write. And that's what Nikhil is doing skillfully in his work. I wish Nikhil, my bro to achieve his dreams and goals. Hard work written on paper and then putting it professionally is hard to do alone from the Valley. But with God's grace and blessings of elders he again wins the heart of his readers and that's what we all wish for him. May God bless him and good comes his way.

{Er. Akhil Mahajan, MBA- Marketing & HR, New Delhi.}

One liner wishes from the Author's family:

Shveta @ It was always expected of Nikhil to be unique and make us proud, his creative individuality was always apparent to us & now shall be to all his readers. Wish him more dreams that he can make come true.

{Currently pursuing PG, Dental Sciences, Muradabad.}

Neha @ To accomplish great things, we must not only act, but also dream, not only plan but also believe. Best wishes for your novel.

{Currently working as Teacher, M. Phil. Commerce, J&K.}

Nandita @ I wish you all kinds of good luck. I'm sprinkles fairy dust on you for even more luck.

{BAMS 3rd yr., Jammu Institute of Ayurveda n' Research , J&K.}

Growing up in a closed atmosphere in a valley of J and K we never knew Nikhil will take such initiatives in his life like this. He many a times mentioned about the book and his writing but we never knew he's so much serious about the book and all the stuff.

But the very day he came up with the e-mail saying he's in contact with publishing house for the publishing work for his first book, we came to know about his serious writing skills. ***"Our best wishes are with him always."***

From brothers, sisters and all members of the Mahajan's Family.

Mails from fans for the previous work:

Akash Sharma@ hi i read ur "my love never faked" its touching story but in the end it is not very clear that weather priya character is real or fake if it is real then now both of u r together or...

Shibu Kataria@ Hi, Nikhil how are you? hope u r fine,,i m shibu frm delhi.i m reading ur novel my love nve faked...this story is too good...its ur real story... aap ki second book kab tak market me aa rhi hai... plz reply if u hve time. bye.. tke care... shibu

Kunal Patil@ If Ur novel MY LOVE NEVER FAKED is imaginary, then how could be Priya is real character. Is PRIYA a real character? How could u leave her sir? OR she leaves u?

Sanaica malhotra@ hiii nikhil..Sanaica dis side. I read ur novel today....I seriously feel dis was a really beautiful love story... I hate reading novel par I don't know why I chose ur novel 2 read n its really gud one... i dnt hv words 2 express hw beautiful love story it is.. thnks 4 writing such a beautiful love story...

Bhanu Gautam@ Hi! Nikhil i read your book and really I like it most; it is very lovely story and also it is the best story book of my life. Congrats to u for ur writing and I want to know that which is ur next book. About love.....plz tell me...... love u, god bless u................BHANU

Mahi kaur @ I am a huge fan of yours. Last month when I went to the book store, your book" My love never faked" caught my eye and i rushed to buy it. When I sat down to read it I finished it at once. The experience was awesome and chilling. i fell in love with the cute, sweet character of "ABHI" instantly. I was wondering if his character is based on any one you know in real life, probably you? My favorite part of the book was the last chapter where Abhi and Priya unite. I had tears in my eyes seeing Abhi unite with the love of his life. I loved your cool style of writing and I was wondering if you are working on a new novel right now.??

And thanks to Shriya, Wadia, Mohit, Heena, Namrita, Shipra, Alisha, Ruhi, Paras, Mughda, Jagruti, Kiran, Mehak, Kasturi, Ajaz, Sheetal, Abhi, Pawan, Vibha Sharma, Divyansh, Nikhil, Vinay Kumar, Sapna, Charu, Payal, Rachna and all my well wishers and fans for mailing me and a heartiest sorry I could not include each and every email here but would like to thank all those who appreciate my work, love to read it.

Keep reading and keep writing.

Thanks to **Deepesh Sharma** and **Vinnie Shetty** for their work on FB with their precious updates. Thanks to Mr. Gandhi, Zankrut, Hitesh for their timely help and wise suggestions.

Glimpse of the previous work:

Abhi always makes a lot of mistakes in his life because of his mischievous attitude and Priya Abhi's Gf always forgives him for all this. She always says that one day she will leave if things keep on repeating like this but being careless to his lady; Abhi never thought that Priya would ever leave him. He keeps on repeating mistakes again and again till the time Priya was completely gone out of his life.

The romantic story "MY LOVE NEVER FAKED..." is about love between Abhi, a last year Physiotherapy student and Priya, MBA student. Both love each other but somehow in the story Ellen, a beautiful American lady, comes between them and Abhi got confused.

He went on with Ellen, date her and get physical with her being drunk and got caught. Abhi tries to reconcile the matter and try to make her understand that he's still innocent from his part and all he was going through was a little confusion about his status in his love life.

And then...

MY LOVE NEVER FAKED... is a bestseller now and is avail all across the country.

EPILOGUE

He was sitting in front of me.

Eye for an eye and many thoughts in my mind...

Me: Why did you do this to me when you are my best friend? You were there with me from the very bad phase to good times of my life. Then why you changed the name of the manuscript, my love story, my life and if you want to get it published with your name then why did you manipulate it before submitting it.

On the table with the cigarette lightened and the beer mug in my hand. With the each sip of the toxicant sliding going down my throat, killing me softly and breaking me into several pieces. I was talking and this was not the only thing that was killing me, the silence of my best friend was killing me more than his written words…

And finally the reply came from the other side:

“No one in this world is interesting enough to be sold out” voice came from the other side.

"You think you are good enough to be read" continued my friend.

"But the things in it have been manipulated"; I said.

"You were not that much interesting, I added just a few lines to make you and your life interesting"; said this little friend of mine to defend himself.

"And what about the names and the feelings"; I question him.

"You ask yourself, you think you can utter everything in this world and anyone cares about it"; the reply was convincing.

The cigarette was still there in my hand, I could feel the smoke but the conversion was deep and the thoughts were convincing this time making it clear something good was done on my part.

I looked down on the table for my mug and raising my head to look up while I picked up the drink. The room was like a hot box full of smoke.

"And Priya"; I asked again with the last word of hope as I cared for her the most.

"And what about those whom you betrayed when she was not around"

Flashes of Diva and Gauri rushed into my mind and a gush of blood entered my heart. My heart pounded for a while.

I took a deep puff; I could feel the smoke of my cigarette entering my lungs and my alveoli passing them to my blood circulation. I look at the other side of the table...

I was left alone with my loneliness... There was no one sitting there. This friend of mine was nothing; just my loneliness and me. It was my consciousness which was not allowing me to manipulate the script. Now it was clear to me that whatever I did, I did for her and since now I am alone with my best friend i.e. myself. I was lost for words but all I could say now is:

"Yes I manipulate it, just to make myself interesting. I am a simple person with simple life, just like any ordinary person out there in this world."

And the level of fulfillment ended this thought that I had robbed myself yet I was satisfied with this feeling. Now I was:

All alone in the crowd...

"As you read now is a fiction story."

Project name

"MY Fckn* AUTOBIOGRAPHY"

Current status of the characters:

A stolen story manipulated and published…

He got the answer and was somewhat convinced... Are you?

Mani in love with Diva confuses himself with Meha….Duh! A love triangle

Meha never forgave Mani for that.

Kabir, Diva's boyfriend…Shit happens

Kabir married and well settled. Diva never talked to him again. It is still unknown what happened between Kabir and Diva that she decided to come back…

Never questioned and never answered…

Karan a true spy friend and the rescuer…

Still spying somewhere helping someone out with his hacking skills and his love crash courses...

Gauri, Mani's senior and Mani's crush….

Mani admits he's under the piles of sacrifice made by Gauri coz that day if Gauri had not compromised, Mani would have been again shipwrecked …

Mani never came to know whether Gauri was there to say yes to Mani or she was helping him out the melodrama.

A teacher… and a mysterious friendship

Mani took his degree anyhow and Miss. Sehgal actually now Mrs. Sehgal is settled down and Mani still chat with her and the friendship remains secretive.

Break-ups and make-ups….A state of confusion

Not a part of life…

Hostel parties…. Friends and a bet

Mani gifted that 10 rupee note to Rahul. He framed that currency and has placed it on the wall next to his certificates and likes to show it to all whenever someone visits his house.

Priya: Still in no contact… And an another novel been put down

Do you think this writer is worth?

www.ingramcontent.com/pod-product-compliance
Ingram Content Group UK Ltd.
Pitfield, Milton Keynes, MK11 3LW, UK
UKHW021700190726
13853UKWH00001B/373

9 789380 349442